Lock Down Publications and Ca$h
Presents

I0680313

BACK IN BLOOD

The Ultimate Sacrifice

Written By

LO-LIFE

First Edition 2025

Printed in the United States of America

This is a work of fiction. Names, characters, places, and incidents either
are products of the author's imagination or are used fictitiously. Any
similarity to actual events or locales or persons, living or dead, is
entirely coincidental.

Lock Down Publications
P.O. Box 944
Stockbridge, GA 30281
www.lockdownpublications.com

Like our page on Facebook: Lock Down Publications
www.facebook.com/lockdownpublications.ldp

Stay Connected with Us!

Text **LOCKDOWN** to 22828 to stay up-to-date with new releases, sneak peaks, contests and more…

Like our page on Facebook:
Lock Down Publications

Join Lock Down Publications/The New Era Reading Group

Visit our website:
www.lockdownpublications.com

Follow us on Instagram:
Lock Down Publications

Email Us: We want to hear from you!

Dedication

What's good y'all? After reading my first couple series, a lot of people got at me about their names not being mentioned. To be honest, sometimes it's just a slip of memory. I always say, if I don't get you on this one, I'll get you on the next.

To Cash and the Lockdown Fam: much love and appreciation for allowing me to paint my pictures on a great stage. For someone in my position, this opportunity is priceless.

To all *The Guys* on that "Freaky Ferg," who read my work and gave me constructive criticism. Y'all let me know, my shit is gas. Straight pressure! Snook aka Lil Antho., work clean young nigga and hold it down. My nigga Tyler LeBlanc aka, T.Y (Jelly). Naw, let me stop playing bro. Like you always say, "It's hard being TY." To my nigga Free World Earl aka EJ, "the one that stamps the tramps," stay up, my nigga; they gone have to let you go one day, and when you do, make them pay for it. To Tito. (Waco). "Have no fear, Tito's here." Stop drinking all them sodas, my nigga. Brian Loud aka. B. Loud. Thank you for all that money you gave me, when I skin your ass up on them bets. LOL. Naw, for real, I ain't never seen a nigga gamble as hard as you do. To D. Rose and Korey G., I'm waiting on y'all to drop some material, so we can co-author something. No one's going to know how live y'all are, unless y'all show them. To X-Man: You got to let up off them niggas. It ain't like it used to be. Boss niggas don't sweat the insignificant. To Tego: I just want you to know, I will always be up one. To Jesse J.: The game's the same, so us Playas should never change. To my old celly Jersey aka Trip, you need to retire, G, we're getting too old for this shit. To all my Hispanic patnas who fucked with the kid, the long way. Ernesto "Tito" Nino. (San Antone stand up) I haven't met to many that are actually who they say they are. You're one of them. Keep your head up G. Edgar: (East Dallas, stand up.) Remember, when you're good to the game, the game's good to you. And when you get something on the G, it ain't free, you paid dues for that. Rudy aka Turtle: I might never meet someone I beat as badly as I beat you in Spades. Lol. One of the realest guys I've come across. Ray Ray: I'll never forget the love you showed, when others turn me away because of politics. For that, you will always be able to pull up.

Now for the ladies. I've pretty much shouted out everyone. Except one. To Dorian A. Taylor, my very *special* friend, confidant, and much more. For years, we've downplayed how much you mean to me. Not anymore. Thank you for all those trips to come see me and those long talks on the phone. I don't think you'll ever know how much it means to me. To my extra son and daughter, Charlotte and Austin aka. Monster Flex Fly, I love y'all like my own. Thank you for bringing your mother joy, and never start it, but when it comes your way, *show that work!*

Well, like I always say if I missed you this go round, I'll try and catch you on the next. My goal is to keep them coming and provide the world with authentic, elaborate, street literature. Until the next time, East up till my feet up. Bombs over Baghdad!

Prologue

"Bro, I don't want to hear that shit. If you believe in them sorry-ass Texans, then put your bread on them," Rashard challenged Kaydon as they all congregated in the small, one-bedroom apartment. Blunts of Loud were being passed around, coffee cups filled with lean placed on the table. The four of them sat back, talking shit and playing *Madden*.

"You know what, that's a bet. What you trynna do?" Kaydon responded.

"Make it light on yourself. We both know that nigga CJ can't fuck with Jalen Hurts." Rashard was team Eastside all the way. Anything that came out of the East, he was with it.

Kaydon thought about it for a second. He wasn't in the habit of fucking off no paper but, "Fuck it, bet a hundred on it," he stated with confidence.

"Bet," Rashard replied before looking at his other two homies, Demon and AD. "What y'all trynna do?" He was feeling himself.

Demon hit the blunt, then blew out the pungent smoke. "Nigga, I don't fuck with neither one of them whack ass niggas. You know I'm Patty Mahomes, all day."

AD scoffed, then chuckled. "Nigga, when you start fucking with Mahomes? Let me find out you another one of them dick-riding, band-wagon-jumping ass niggas. Matter of fact, I bet you can't even tell me what college he went to."

Demon looked confused. "Man, I don't give a fuck what college he went to. I *know* he gets a nigga paid. I'm riding with the money."

AD shook his head. "Nigga, you out of there."

The four of them had been friends most of their lives. Kaydon was twenty-eight years old, and therefore the oldest. At six foot, two, two hundred and twenty pounds, with a short temper, he would often be the most intimidating. He was smooth with his hands and wouldn't hesitate to buss his gun. But his talent came with his mental capacity, along with his supreme hustling skills.

Rashard was his right-hand man. It had been that way ever since they were in elementary. Their mothers, Lavella and Linda, had been best friends, since before the boys had been born. So, Kaydon and Rashard were more like brothers—brothers who were nothing alike.

Where Kaydon was tall, with a copper-red skin tone, Rashard—or Rah, as they called him—was five foot ten, a hundred and ninety pounds, with a Hershey-type complexion. Kaydon was a natural born hustler and could sell just about anything. Rah was a bully. He would rob and steal to get his. Even though they were completely different, their friendship withstood the test of time.

Damon, a.k.a. *Demon*, was another case altogether. At twenty-five years old, he was the youngest of the group. At five foot eleven, two hundred and forty pounds, he was considered the young bull of the crew. He rarely said much when strangers were among them. With skin as black as asphalt, and eyes that seemed red and irritated at all times, it was no wonder how he got the moniker, Demon. Not to mention, he was a complete monster when it came time to slide on an op.

At fifteen years old, Demon moved to the East. He'd gotten into some beef with a notorious Crip named Crazy Loc. Right there in the middle of the apartments, Demon drew down and shot Crazy Loc in the head. Crazy stayed on life support for two months. Finally, they decided to pull the plug. Since Demon had just moved into the apartments, no one really knew who he was. When the cops came, they couldn't identify the shooter.

Shortly after, a few of Crazy's homeboys tried to catch Demon lacking. Kaydon peeped the play and pulled up to the rescue. Ever since then, Demon had been a permanent fixture of the crew. Ten years later, he was still there.

AD, the last member of the crew, was the pretty boy of the clique. A high-yellow nigga with a good grade of reddish-brown hair, at six foot even and a hundred and ninety pounds, he stayed at the gym at least three or four times a week. AD was the type that stayed around a female, while his baby momma Andrea was the freak of the week. He'd been knowing Kaydon and Rah since they attended Cunningham Middle School together. All in all, the four of them were like brothers, and they'd been to hell and back for each other.

Kaydon felt his phone vibrate and pulled it out of his pocket. He checked the screen and saw it was his little side piece, Keeda, calling. He smiled at the thought of all the freaky shit he had in store for her.

Keeda was a five-foot-six redbone from the Southwest who loved to suck dick and take it up her big ol' booty. Even though Kaydon had a bad bitch at home, he couldn't resist the urge to slide in something new every now and then. He pressed answer and put the phone to his ear. "Hello?"

"Hey, daddy, when you coming through?"

"I'm 'bout to leave now," Kaydon said as he began to grab his weed, lighter, and cigarettes off the coffee table.

"Can you please hurry your ass up? My pussy so fucking wet right now. I need a dose of that big-ass dick you got carrying around."

That brought a laugh out of Kaydon.

"Calm down, lil' momma. Trust and believe, you gone get all you can eat."

"Hmm huh," she moaned into his ear. Kaydon's dick twitched. He knew he had to get to that cat ASAP. He covered the phone with his left hand so she wouldn't hear him talking to the fellas.

"Say, AD, play for me. I'm 'bout to shoot over to Keeda's spot. If Danielle pulls up looking for me, just tell her y'all ain't see me none today." Danielle was his girl, who should have been his baby momma, but she had a miscarriage when they were both twenty. They'd been together for ten years, and even though Kaydon stepped out from time to time, he loved her dirty drawers.

AD grabbed the controller, looked up, and said, "Come on, nigga. What you think we 'bout to tell her? Oh yeah, he went to fuck his side bitch? Bro, you tripping. Just make sure you leave that hundred, just in case I can't get it done with these sorry-ass Texans."

Kaydon tossed the hundred on the table, then made his way out the door. "Yeah, yeah. Whatever, nigga," Kaydon said as he stepped outside and closed the door behind him. There was a slight chill in the air.

Dressed in a red-and-white striped Polo shirt, red Polo shorts, and a pair of red-and-white Valentine's Day Jordans, you could tell what Kaydon's affiliation was from a mile away. He made his way to the parking lot, about to jump in his burnt-orange, ninety-six Chevy Impala SS on eighty-four swangers, when he noticed a black Ford SUV pulling up.

He cursed himself for leaving his Glock under the driver's seat. He just hoped it wasn't them Pleasantville niggas they'd been beefing with. He peered into the front windshield of the SUV. Two white boys were seated in front. Then it dawned on him. Rashard had said earlier he had two white boys coming through. Supposedly, they were trying to spend ten bands on two k-packs of Percs. Knowing Rashard, they were going to leave with no pills and ten thousand dollars poorer.

"Aye, say bro," the driver yelled from the safety of the truck.

Kaydon turned his head while reaching in his pocket for his keys. "Wassup?"

"Do you know Rambo?"

Rambo was Rah's alias when he was up to no good. Nobody knew Rashard as Rambo except for the clique and his victims. By them asking for that name, Kay already knew the business.

"Naw, homie. I don't know any Rambo." Now he was trying to get off the scene before shit got ugly. As he hopped in his slab, he saw Rashard walk up to the SUV. After a few short words, he saw the white boys park and hop out of their truck. Kaydon backed out of the parking space and made his way to the Southwest.

As he drove, his phone began to vibrate. He picked it up and saw it was Danielle calling. He let it go to voicemail. He already knew she was going to give him an earful when he came home. So, *fuck it!* Right now, he needed to focus on getting some of that grade-A top and bottom from Keeda.

An Hour Later:

Slurp. Slurp. Sluurrrpppp!

Kaydon sat on the bed, back against the headboard, legs spread wide, feet flat on the mattress. Keeda, on her hands and knees between his thighs, devoured his nine-inch dick. She kept him sloppy and wet. Saliva dripped down his shaft as she sucked and stroked him. Kay's eyes locked on the top of her head, and every pull of her lips sent a shiver through his cock.

Keeda grabbed him at the base, pushing her head further into his lap, trying her best to deep throat the whole thing. Kaydon's head hit the wall as he groaned in pleasure. "OH shit. Damn, girl. Suck that dick."

She moaned around his rod while reaching between her thighs and flicking at her clit. "Fuck, Keeda. I'm 'bout to cum."

She popped him out of her mouth. "Cum down my throat, baby. Fill my stomach up."

Kay grabbed the back of her head and humped into her mouth. Globs of creamy nut spat forth from the tip of his dick. He could feel her swallow his seeds. His nuts jumped for joy, eager to give her more.

Keeda pulled down on the skin and sucked gently on the head, kissing the tip as Kaydon sat back, breathless. "Damn, baby, I missed this dick," she moaned as she jacked him off slowly.

Once he was back primed up, Keeda pulled him by his thighs until he was lying flat on his back. With his dick straight in the air, she straddled him. She looked into his eyes, leaned forward, and kissed him passionately. Kaydon could taste the faint trace of his semen on her tongue. She had him turnt out.

As Keeda lightly bit on his bottom lip, she reached back and stuffed him into her oven. Her pussy felt super wet and warm. To be such a freak, her coochie was always tight as hell. Kaydon grabbed ahold of her fleshy, plump ass cheeks, kneading them like dough as she began to work the hips. Her cunt juice poured out of her snatch profusely, drenching his balls as she bounced up and down onto his lap.

Clap. Clap. Clap. Her big ol' booty crashed into the tops of his thighs, the bottom of her cheeks slapping against his ball sack. Kaydon grabbed her around the waist for leverage. After he was secured, he began to punish her coochie.

"Oh yes. Oh yes. Fuck, baby. This dick is all in my chest," she screamed as she placed her face in the crux of his neck.

Kay grabbed the back of her head with his right hand as he continued to pop his hips, digging her guts out. "You love this dick, baby?"

"Oh, yes, daddy. I love this dick!"

"If you love this dick, your ass better cum on it. You hear me? Your ass better cum on this dick, you nasty-ass bitch. Right the fuck now!" Kaydon growled.

11

Hearing him call her a nasty-ass bitch did it. With a loud roar, Keeda proclaimed her arrival. "Oh shit. Fuck me, I'm cumming! I'm cumming! I'm cummmminnnggg!"

Her body shook and vibrated. Her walls snatched at his cock. He felt her warm liquid dribble over his pelvic area and pour onto the bed.

She huffed into his ear as she struggled to regain her composure. "Huh. Huh. Whew. Boy, with a dick like that, a bitch could live happily ever after just being your side bitch."

Instead of responding, Kaydon chuckled, then popped his hips, causing Keeda to moan. She bit her lip, shook her head, then held on as Kay fucked her into oblivion.

At 4:12 a.m., Kaydon walked through the front door of the apartment he shared with his longtime girlfriend. Danielle Crowder was one of the baddest females on the East. At five foot three, a hundred and thirty-two pounds, c-cup breasts and a thirty-eight-inch ass, she was what they called built for fucking!

Danielle and Kay began messing around when they were seniors in high school. They'd met one night at a kickback Danielle's homegirl Quita was having. At the time, Danielle was seeing this cat from across town, who happened to be at the party. Kay found a way to lure her away from her dude. They exchanged numbers, linked up the next night, and the rest was history.

Kaydon already knew he was about to hear her mouth. He didn't relish it, but he understood. If he wanted to keep Danielle, he had to put up with certain shit—and her mouth was one of them. Soon as he stepped foot into the bedroom, she arose from the bed like the Undertaker. Nothing on but a red thong.

"Nigga, where the fuck you been?"

"I was with my relative Tater." Kaydon knew she hated Tater more than anybody else in the world. No matter what was going on, she would never call him. And if she did, he would never answer.

"You a motherfucking lie, nigga. Come here."

Kay already knew what the deal was. She wanted to smell his dick, but he was one step ahead. He figured she would have been suspicious if he came in smelling like soap, so before he came home, he showered at Keeda's, then jogged around the apartments for ten minutes. That way, his nuts would be nice and sweaty.

He fought to hide the smirk as she pulled at his waistband, nearly popping the button on his Polo shorts. After she unzipped him, she reached in and fished out his dick. She felt how heavy it was, and her clit began to thump. She peered at him, squinting her eyes, before leaning over to sniff at it. After inhaling three good times, she released her grip and let it fall, watching as his dick flopped and smacked against his thigh.

Kaydon looked down at her with a condescending smirk. "Uh huh. What it smell like?"

Danielle looked away.

"Oh, you ain't got shit to say now, do you? You know the rule. If you pull that motherfucker out and it doesn't smell like pussy, you know what you gotta do."

Danielle frowned her face up. "Nigga, you want me to suck your sweaty-ass dick?"

"Hell yeah! You accused a nigga of cheating. You outta line for that. So, to make it up, I need my dick sucked and my sweaty-ass balls licked."

Danielle looked at his python. She took a deep breath, grabbed ahold of it, and began to stroke it. Within seconds, Kay was at full salute. She opened her mouth up wide and did exactly what he said he needed her to do—suck his dick and lick his sweaty-ass balls.

Two Weeks Later:

It was a hot, humid, Saturday afternoon. The clock read 12:40 p.m. The sun was on *fuck-the-world!* Kay was at the carwash on Wallisville, shining up his Impala. He grabbed his phone out the front seat and hit Rashard up to see what was taking him so long. He needed some Percs, and Rah was supposed to shoot him a hundred of them, for the low.

As he sat in the driver seat, opened the door with his left foot hanging out, he went ahead and texted Keeda also—trying to see what she had planned for later that night. He heard the loud bass of someone's stereo system and instantly knew it was Rashard—courtesy of the six, twelve-inch subwoofers he kept locked away in his cocaine white, '76 Lincoln Continental. Even from a hundred yards away, he could hear Moneybag Yo rapping about how he never ran from a nigga.

Just as Keeda texted back, letting him know she had nothing planned and he could come through, two unmarked cars and three patrol vehicles swooped into the carwash. It took a second for Kaydon to realize they were there for him. By then, it was too late to make a move. As they put him in cuffs and attempted to place him in the back of the car, he spotted Rah across the street, posted at the corner store. They locked eyes and Rashard mouthed, *"Don't worry, I got you."* Kaydon nodded in acknowledgement and gratitude, right before they stuffed him into the back and closed the door on his freedom.

Chapter 1

Kaydon

I just got booked in for two aggravated robberies, and don't know what the fuck is going on. As soon as I get on the last floor of intake, I call my bitch Danielle. She answers immediately. "Hello?"

"Wassup, D?"

"Nigga, what the fuck is going on? Rah came by earlier, talking 'bout they snatched you up at the carwash."

"Yeah, that's facts. They talking 'bout two agg robberies. Babe. No cap. On me, I don't know what they're talking 'bout."

"Well, what you need me to do?"

"Really, right now it's too early. I need to see if they give me a bond. If it's reasonable, then I'ma pop that hoe."

"Where's your car at?"

"That's the thing. I don't know if they impounded my shit or what. I need you to locate it, so if they did, you can get my shit out, ASAP. The longer it sits in there, the more they gone try an' charge a nigga."

"You know what, Imma ask Rah, if he saw them tow it."

"Where that nigga at anyway?"

"I don't know. He just left. He said. He came straight over here to tell me they took you to jail."

Something clicked, but I couldn't put my finger on it. I looked at the time—*4:15 p.m.* "Look, baby, I don't know how long a nigga will be in intake, but soon as I make it to the floor, I'ma call you."

"Do you have any money on your books?"

"Oh yeah. I got thirty-two hundred on me. As soon as they give me a bond, you can come grab it." I wasn't sure how long before they'd give me bail, so until then, it was only the bare necessities.

"Okay, babe. Damn, this some fucked-up shit."

I could tell Danielle was afraid of the outcome. Since we'd been together, I never did more than a couple months in the county. I loved getting money too much to commit anything aggravated. Most of my charges were drug-related.

"It's gotta be some type of explanation. You and I both know I don't do no robbing. It must be a case of mistaken identity." We rode on the phone a little longer, then they called my name for medical, so we hung up.

Once medical was done with me, instead of calling Danielle back, I called the guys. I needed to lace them up. The first call I made was to my day one.

"Hello?"

"Wassup, Rah?"

"My nigga, what the fuck you got going on?"

"Blood. No cap, I don't know what this shit about. I was waiting for you at the carwash when them hoes just swooped in. They talking 'bout, two aggravated robberies."

"Say what?"

"Exactly. You know I don't even be on that type of time."

"Ova stood. Damn, what your bond looking like?"

"I ain't got one yet, but I know that bitch liable to be high as hell."

"Well, look, Blood, just let me know what the deal is, and we'll patch up if need be."

"A'ight, well—" I was about to hang up, but as an afterthought, I remembered to ask, "You talked to Danielle?"

"Uh . . . Yeah. I had swung through and laced her up on everything. She said she'll come see you as soon as you get on the floor."

"When was this?" I don't know why it mattered to me, but it did.

"Shit. That was way earlier. I pulled up on her right after they snatched you up. I was over there probably ten minutes." Something was nagging at my subconscious. It was like looking at a puzzle, but not knowing that a piece was missing.

"A'ight, Blood. That's a bet. I'll hit y'all niggas when I touch the floor."

"Bet that, Blood. Love, nigga."

"Love." I hung the phone up with him, then called AD.

"Hello?"

A female voice answered his phone. I knew it was his ratchet-ass baby momma, Andrea. She was a real cool chick to kick it with, but by no means was she wifey material. I used to see her at her job every now and then. She worked in the electronics department. I don't think there was a time I went up there, she wasn't in a different nigga's face. At first, I used to lace my nigga up about it. I guess whatever excuse she gave him worked. Either he didn't care, or he didn't believe it. So, I just stopped mentioning it.

"Say, Drea, is that nigga AD around?"

"He in the shower right now."

"Of course. I know he wouldn't go for you answering his phone," I stated, honestly.

"Boy, boo. I'll answer this nigga's phone whenever I get goddamn ready to."

She knows that's straight cap. My nigga would go across her shit if he caught her going through his phone.

"A'ight. Whatever. When that nigga get out the shower, tell him they locked me up for some bullshit. Talking 'bout two aggravated robberies."

"Damn, nigga. You taking niggas' shit now?" This nothing-ass broad had the nerve to ask me.

"Didn't you just hear me say, it's some bullshit." I honestly don't see what my nigga sees in this trash-ass thot. Yeah, she's fine as fuck, with a nasty-ass walk. So, I'm guessing the pussy is good. Other than that, she ain't got shit else working for her.

"Pssht." She smacked her lips. "Look, Imma let him know you called and deliver your message when he gets out the shower, but I don't appr—" *Click.* I hung up in her face before she could finish her sentence. I seriously don't know how the homie does it.

Next, I called the lil' homie, Demon. He didn't answer, so I called my big bro, Harrell. I really didn't want to, but I know for a big bond, I might need collateral. He's the only one I know that could help me with that. He answered the phone with an attitude.

"What you done did now, nigga?"

"Come on, bro, why you just automatically assume I did something?"

"Because, you're calling me from jail, nigga. Duh." It's like, he forgets where he comes from. Now that he makes close to a hundred bands a year, the nigga acts like he was born with money. Like he hasn't seen what our people go through.

"Bro, yo' act like innocent niggas don't go to jail, or something."

He snorts. "I never did. And what are they saying you did?"

"Aggravated Robbery."

"Say, check it out little brother. I been told you . . ." he trailed off mid-sentence. There was a murmur in the background, like someone was speaking to him. "Say what? It's Kaydon."

There was a brief pause before my big bro continued: "Say, Claudia said hi."

"Tell her I said wassup."

"Claudia, he said wassup. Anyway, what was I saying? Oh yeah. I been told your ass to stop playing and get a job. But, you still want to be in the streets selling dope. Now, they talking 'bout you taking people's shit."

I pinch the bridge of my nose and shake my head. My big brother Harrell could be so extra sometimes. The nigga used to be knee-deep in the streets when he was younger, but his best friend got his face blown off for a nine-piece, and that scared my brother straight. At twenty-five years old, he got all the way out the way.

He landed a job at the Port of Houston, and now that he's thirty-five, he's got a crib, a couple cars, and a badass Colombian wife named Claudia. I sit back and let him preach because I know I will need him. After he gets done ranting, I tell him that I may need help if my bond is too high. He scoffs at me.

"Nigga, I'm not fucking my bread off on no motherfucking bond. You made your bed, now go lie in it."

I grip the receiver so tight, my knuckles turn white. I wanted so bad to give him a piece of my mind, but I held my tongue. This is some serious shit, and I know I'll need him, so I just replied, "A'ight, bro." Then, I hung up the phone. I sat back and tried to make sense of everything. I don't do drugs that would make me black out and forget a whole robbery charge. I don't know what else it could be.

After sitting there for an hour, I decided to call Keeda's ass.

"Hello?"

"Hey, baby girl."

"Kaydon? What the fuck?"

"Yeah. Them hoes got me on some bullshit, but Imma beat it. You gone come up here and fuck with a nigga or what?" I honestly didn't think she would. Even though we'd been fucking for some time, I didn't think I gave her enough of me to warrant her to ride out the time with a nigga. If she did, it'd be a pleasant surprise.

"Of course, baby. Soon as you get housed, let me know. I'll catch the bus up there." Bless her heart. Besides sex, she really ain't have shit to offer. At twenty-three, she was too damn old to be catching the bus. Especially to go see a nigga in jail.

"That's a bet, baby, I'll be waiting on you." I hung the phone up. Now, for the call that I'd been dreading. My momma. Lavella Snow was a character and a half. She had my brother when she was fifteen and me when she was twenty-two. Like my pops, she was in the streets. She used to sell a lil dope and set niggas up to get robbed. She even started stripping when pops went to jail, so she could take care of herself, my brother, and me. So, according to her, a nigga couldn't get by her with nothing.

"Hello?"

"Hey, momma."

"Boy, don't hey momma me. What you got going on?"

"What you mean?"

"Linda already told me. Your ass got picked up for something."

Linda was my mom's best friend, who is also my best friend Rashard's momma. They'd been best friends since they were kids. Anything my mom did, Ms. Linda did also. And vice versa. Ms. Linda even told me some of her old stripper stories when my momma wasn't around. To be fifty years old, she was still fine as hell.

Five foot six, a hundred and fifty pounds, double-D titties, with a super fat ass. Quiet as kept, she was also a stone cold freak. Not to say I'd ever fuck with her. Her stories would always leave my dick harder than Chinese calculus. But, I couldn't cross that line, even if I wanted to. That's how Rashard and I had been so close growing up. Our mothers were like sisters.

"Yeah, momma. They came and snatched me up. Talking 'bout two aggravated robberies."

"I know you already know this, but don't tell them people nothing."

"Momma, you know I don't deal with no swine, but Imma need a lawyer."

"Damn, baby, I just fucked off my income tax. I got your daddy a parole lawyer. You know, he's about to come up. Twenty-six years flat."

My pops got fifty years for an M, but caught a deuce for a cell phone. They gave him a one-year setoff.

"Let me see what I can come up with."

I know that really meant, *you're shit out of luck*. We finished our conversation, and I waited for them to call my name.

"Snow? Kaydon Snow?" I stood up and walked towards classification. They slapped a green armband on me. I looked at the housing assignment: 7 M 2.

Danielle (Earlier that day):

"Girl, what you mean he didn't check that hoe? Alison, you better tell Chance, Imma fuck his ass up. How he gone let that bum ass bitch push up on him, while you were in the restroom?" I asked my lil sister Alison. She's been having boy problems. I can't call them man problems, because even though they're both nineteen, I still couldn't look at them as a man and woman.

Chance and my sister had been dating since she left for college. He was a six-foot, five-inch boy, in a grown man's body. Even though I hate to admit it, I've seen that boy's package, and he's definitely swanging and banging. Not on no sneaky shit. I woke up one morning and accidentally walked in on him and my sister fucking last summer when they came to my apartment. She was riding him, hard and fast. Soon as I walked in, his extra long dick fell out of her pussy. Before she got a chance to slip it back in, I got an eyeful.

Apparently, they'd gone out to eat, and while my sister was in the restroom, some college junior thot pulled up trying to get Chance's number. Luckily, my sister had forgotten to grab her wipes. When she came out, she caught Ms. Thot all in her nigga's smiling face. "He said I didn't give him a chance to. That ole girl literally pulled up on him, five seconds before I came out."

My sister was always trying to find a technicality to save his ass. The dick must be superb. I was about to go in on her ass when I heard my line beep. I looked at the phone and saw a text message from my man's best friend, Rashard.

Rashard: *I'm outside. Cum open the door.*

I wonder what he wants. I put the phone back up to my ear and told Alison I'd call her back. I contemplated getting dressed because I was wearing one of Kaydon's wife beaters and a pair of red boy shorts that were cutting into my creases. I walked by the full-length mirror and could clearly see my sex lips poking out the side of the crotch band. I stuck my finger between the elastic, and with a "pop," I pulled the material out the crack of my pussy. I opened the door, turned around, and let Rashard in.

Without looking back, I knew he was staring at my ass. "Kaydon isn't here," I tell him, over my shoulder. I knew he already knew that. Those two motherfuckers are joined at the hip. They don't do anything without the other one knowing about it. If I didn't know any better, I'd think they were fucking.

"Yeah, I know. He just got locked up." I stopped dead in my tracks and snapped my head around.

"What?" I know I just didn't hear what I think I did.

"Yeah. He was at the carwash waiting on me. Soon as I was about to turn in, I saw all types of laws run down on him," Rah informed me.

I couldn't believe what I was hearing. "Do you know what for?"

"Hell naw. You know Kaydon don't do shit but grind. The way they pulled up, it was like he murdered somebody."

My knees got weak. I began to get lightheaded. I needed to sit down. As long as we'd been together, Kaydon had never done serious time. The most was a few months in the county. I sat down on the loveseat so I could think clearly. I prayed it wasn't anything serious. I don't know what I would do if he was taken away from me.

I was so lost in my thoughts, I almost forgot Rah was in the apartment with me. I felt his eyes staring a hole in me, and I realized I was sitting with my legs gapped open, as if I was braiding someone's hair. I looked into his eyes and saw the hunger. Then my eyes traveled south and landed on the unmistakable bulge in the front of his jeans. I wet my lips.

He must have smelled my need because he took three steps, while unzipping his jeans and pulling out his eight-inch slab of meat. Without so much as one word between us, I reached up and grabbed ahold of his cock. It felt so hot and heavy in my tiny little hands. Kaydon had him on length, but Rashard was a little more thicker.

I know a lot of people might be like, *Damn, she's fucking her man's best friend?* That bitch is out of there. They might be right. What, you don't think I know Kaydon's stepping out on me? So it's cool for him to do it, but I can't?

Rashard started tapping this ass when he exposed Kaydon for the lying cheater he was. I was at home alone, blowing his phone up. He'd claimed that he was with his no-good cousin Tater, so I called Rashard to see if he had heard from him. I could tell Rah was lit. At first, he didn't even recognize who I was. Then, before I knew it, he was at my front door. I still don't know why he did it, but he called Kaydon, right there in front of me, and let me listen to him brag about how he was about to have a threesome with two stank-ass sisters.

To say I was hurt was an understatement. I'll be the first to admit, I lashed out. I wanted to hurt Kaydon, like he hurt me. So, right there in my living room, I dropped down to my knees and sucked his best friend's dick, until the nigga screamed he was in love with me. Afterwards, I let him fuck me all over the crib. Including the bed Kaydon and I shared. Just to be petty, I didn't wash the sheets. So, when Kaydon finally brought his no-good, lying ass home, I took solace knowing he was sleeping in the sex juices me and his best friend created. That was eight months ago. Since then, Rashard and I have fucked more times than I could count.

I felt my jaw pop, widen to capacity, as I crammed into my mouth. Inch by delicious inch. I inhaled his scent and my coochie's lips became slick with dew. His cock head felt spongy, as I felt it glide against my tongue. He pushed forward and tapped the back of my throat. With his dick in my mouth and trapped between my lips, I used my hands to work his jeans the rest of the way down. Once he stepped out of them, his balls hung free like mangoes on a tree. I grabbed them with my left hand, kneading them slowly, as my right hand gripped his left ass cheek. He knew I liked to get my face fucked. Especially after receiving bad news. It's nothing like a good, hard skull fuck to keep your problems at bay.

Rashard placed his right foot on the couch next to me. Both hands gripped the sides of my head as he gave me what I needed. His balls swung wildly, tapping my chin. I struggled to breathe. His wide cock clogged my throat. *Awka, awka, awka.* The sound of me choking had my pussy on fire. My clit felt like it was the size of a Mike-N-Ike. Spit flew from the corners of my mouth, dripping down my chin, wetting up my couch cushion.

I became light-headed from the lack of oxygen to my brain, but I wouldn't dare tell him to stop. I was going to suck this nigga's dick until he tapped out or I blacked out. Just when I thought I was on the brink of unconsciousness,

Rashard pulled back. I gasped, taking in a huge, great big gulp of air.

My chest felt as if it were on fire, but my pussy just had its first orgasm of the night. He looked down at me as if I were a disgrace. "Turn that ass around." I quickly obeyed. With my hand planted on the couch cushion and my ass in the air, Rashard peeled my boy shorts down. I could smell how wet I was. The cool air tickled my clit.

Instead of taking them all the way off, he placed them right below my knees. Rah tapped my inner thigh, instructing me to spread them wider. I obliged. I felt him slide his plum-sized cock head up and down my slippery slit. I moaned in anticipation. The heat from my snatch reached up and snapped at his dick. He eased in, then out slowly, teasing me until I begged to be stuffed.

"Rah, pleeaaseee. I need to fuck this pain away. Daddy, please." I damn near cried, like a spoiled brat that'd gotten her favorite doll taken away.

Without warning, he eased past my meaty sex lips and slammed deep into my box. "Awwwww fuuucccckk!" I cried out as I came all over his cock and balls with the first stroke. My knees threatened to give out. I edged forward, planting them on the couch cushion. With my face stuffed into the couch, as if I'm looking for loose change, Rah gripped my hips, dug his feet into the carpet, and pounded my coochie loose. *Squish, squish, squish, squish.* My wetness could be heard all through the apartment.

My booty cheeks crashed against his abs. *Clap, clap, clap.* I can hear him grunting. I feel his dick harden within my walls as my pussy muscles grip him tightly. "Oh shit. Here it comes, D... Fuck, I'm finna nut!" His shaft jerks, and his pipe's about to bust.

I reached back and spread my cheeks apart, exposing my tight, crinkly asshole. He knows what I want. With a loud roar, he pulled out, jacked his dick a few times, aimed, and released his baby batter all up and down my chocolate valley.

The warm, gooey substance slid down my crack as I trembled with glee. I pushed my forefinger into my asshole, making sure it was well-lubricated with cum. Rah reached back and slapped my right booty cheek. *SMACK!* My ass wobbled and stung just a bit. "Damn, D, you got the best pussy. Hands down! A nigga won't ever get tired of this box," he professed.

I turned around, grabbed his piece, and lightly placed kisses all over his crown. What he doesn't know is that for the last eight months, I've been doing my best shit all over town. Everywhere, but the East. Now, instead of Danielle, they started calling me Freaky Dee. I even go by Deenesha in some circles. I spent the next couple of hours showing Rah why I deserve that nickname. As soon as he leaves, I get that free call from *Harris County Jail*. I steady my breathing and accept the call from my man, and the love of my life, Kaydon.

Chapter 2

Rashard

I took a deep breath and hopped inside my triple black, Dodge Charger. My balls still feel sticky after the three-hour session I just had with Danielle. I shake my head and just can't believe how good that pussy is. The crazy thing is it seems like her box gets better and better every time. My engine came alive, and I peeled out of the apartments.

As I'm riding down Uvalde, nostalgia takes a hold of me. These were the same blocks I played hide and go seek on. Then, it was hide and go get it. Then, it was straight *go getting*. Hustling, for days at a time.

My phone vibrates. It's a message from Danielle.

Danielle: *I'm on da phone wit Kay rite now*
Rah: *Hit me when u get off*

I'll admit. I do feel kind of fucked up for fucking my best friend's bitch. Kay and I have been friends since we came out the womb. *Literally!* You might as well say, we're brothers. To be honest, I didn't intend on fucking his girl; that shit just happened.

She called me one night while I was drunk and lit, asking me If I saw Kay. Next thing I know, I'm at her house putting eight inches of dick up in her. That shit was so good, I couldn't stop even if I wanted to.

I know a lot of people might classify me as a fuck nigga, but y'all ain't seen Danielle. Then, sometimes when I used to be over there chillin' with Kay, she'd walk around with a tank top, no bra, and some boy shorts. Ass hanging out the bottom of them motherfuckers. It had been many times I had to run out that bitch with a hard-on.

My phone rang. I looked at the screen and saw a number I didn't recognize. I had an idea of who it was. "Hello?"

"Wassup, Rah?" Kay had already made it to the second floor of intake. That shit was crazy, how twelve just swopped in and snatched my nigga up. He tells me he has two aggravated robberies, and I know it has to be some type of mistake. One thing about Kay, he isn't for the jack game. His cup of tea is quarters, halves, and wholes.

He tells me how he just talked to Danielle. An image of her on the couch, sucking my dick, pops into my head. I damn near zone out while thinking about it. I know I need to stop fucking his girl before he finds out. But I don't know how to. Every time I tell myself Imma fall back, I lay eyes on that fat ass, them juicy tits, that pretty pink pussy, and that's a wrap.

As I'm just getting off the phone with Kay, I pulled up to my T-Lady's crib. Before I hung up, I promised him once he gets a bond, me and the "Guys" will come and get him out. Even though I'm knocking his girl down, that's still my bro and I don't want to see him locked up.

I walk into my momma's crib and smell her in the kitchen doing what she does best: cook! My stomach instantly begins to growl. After that intense round of sex, my appetite is back with a vengeance. My mom hears me come in and calls me to the kitchen.

"Rah Rah, come in here a minute. I need a favor."

My intention was to hop in the shower and wash away the scent of sex, but I head into the kitchen instead. I find her standing over the stove, frying what looks like chicken. To be fifty, she's still the most beautiful woman I know. Standing five foot six, cocoa butter skin tone, a hundred and fifty-three pounds, my momma still had a hell of a figure.

Add that to the fact she still thought she was young, and she was a headache to keep up with.

I had to always get onto her about wearing certain shit around my niggas. For example, right then, she had on some brown tights that were all up in her crack, and one of my shirts I wore when I was twelve years old. Her double D's were trying to bust out, like a nigga with a fresh LWOP.

"Wassup, momma?" I say, as I hugged and kissed her on the cheek.

She takes one whiff and scrunches her face up. "Boy, whose coochie you've been jumping in and out of?"

I look at her crazy. "Huh? What you mean?"

"What you mean, what I mean? You smell like a gallon of coochie. You need to take your ass in that bath, but first, I need to borrow two hundred dollars."

My shoulders slumped. One thing about Linda Manning—she never paid you back. Ever. Well, at least not to her son.

I dug in my pocket and pulled out the smaller knot. If she saw the bigger one, that two hundred might've turned into five hundred, quickly. I carefully peeled off twenties, tens, fives, and even a few ones. I needed to drive home the fact I don't have any more money.

She grabbed the cash, then stuck it in the waistband of her tights. "Now, take your nasty ass in that tub, and your plate will be ready when you get out."

"A'ight, momma."

I shook my head and made my way to the back of the house, to my old room. I moved out of my mom's crib years ago but still come back almost every day to shower, eat, and sometimes just kick it with her. I kept some of my clothes, as well as most of my jewelry, at her spot. I was an only child, so I knew I'd always have a place to lay my head when the streets proved to be too much and I needed a break.

After I hopped out of the shower, I sat and ate with my T-Lady. I told her what happened with Kay, and she immediately hopped on the phone and called his momma. That was expected.

As she chatted away, gossiping about this and that, I went into my room and called the squad up.

AD was arguing with his ratchet-ass baby momma once again, and Demon was helping his uncle do something. I laced them both up about Kay getting snatched up, then I called Danielle.

She said she'd just gotten out of the shower after talking to Kay. We both knew what we was doing was out of line, but the sex was crazy good. I told her when bro got housed on the floor, we could go up there together to see him. After that, we spent the next thirty minutes reminiscing about the session we had earlier that day.

AD

"A'ight, bitch. Keep playing with me. You gone make me buss you in your shit," I told my stupid-ass baby momma, as she threatened to set my clothes on fire. I'm in the garage, standing in my black and red *Polo* boxers, watching her throw the last of my things into a pile. The dumb-ass bitch had a bottle of lighter fluid in her hand, and she keeps acting as if she wants to douse my shit with it.

The whole beef started the night before. I came home after kicking it with the homies, pulled into the apartments, and spotted a black *Maserati* parked near my usual parking spot. I'd been staying in *Deerwood Pines* for the last five years and knew every car that was supposed to be in there. That Ratti wasn't one of them. So, my antennas went up. Something told me to play it safe.

Instead of parking in my usual spot, I parked a little way down and just watched. I texted my baby momma and told her I was on the way home. Sure enough, fifteen seconds later I watched her trifling ass hop out the passenger seat of the car. She had on a burgundy sundress, with some flip-flops on. I shook my head.

I honestly don't know why I continued to fuck with this thot. Maybe it was the fact we had a four-year-old son together. *AJ* was my pride and joy. With copper-tone skin and reddish-brown hair, he was a spitting image of me. I loved him with every fiber of my body.

Truthfully, Andrea getting pregnant was never in the plans. We met at one of the homies, *G Dub's*, birthday party. No cap, the bitch is bad. At five foot four, a hundred and thirty pounds, B-cups and an ass that could swallow up a G-string, *Drea* was one of the baddest chicks in the hood.

I didn't know it at the time I was popping her, but apparently, she had more bodies than a cemetery. By the time I'd found out, I was head over heels in love with her.

Anyway, after I watched her hop out of the *Maserati*, I decided to be petty. Instead of going straight home, I took a detour and ended up at our neighbor *Cassandra's* crib. It had been a while since I'd slid up in her, and I needed a quick tightening up. Drea and *Cassi* were the type of females that pretended they liked each other in public, but behind closed doors, they couldn't stand one another. I know Drea suspected I was fucking Cassi, but could never prove it. I texted Cassi to see what she had going on. Of course, nothing.

I made sure I parked my whip on the other side of the apartments, then walked to her crib. As soon as she answered the door, she knew the deal.

"We don't have much time," I said.

She was cool with just topping me off. After she swallowed my baby batter, I let her ride my face and swallowed her nut, like she did mine.

Twenty minutes later, I was walking in my crib, just as Andrea was bringing her trifling ass out the shower.

"Hey, baby," she coo'd, while applying her scented lotion. She sat back on the bed, with her legs wide and her pussy, puffy, red, and slick. Glistening with her natural essence.

"Wassup?" I replied, as I began to get undressed. My first mind was to hop in the shower. But, as I stood there staring at her sex lips, my dick began to stiffen. No matter how much of a freak she was, my baby momma always seemed to have that snap back.

"Come here," I told her while dropping my boxers. My heavy dick flopped out. Without any words being exchanged, Drea stood up, walked towards me, and sunk down onto her knees.

I looked down at her as she picked my cock up and suspiciously sniffed at it. A slight frown graced her face, but she didn't say anything. Instead, she dipped her head under my hanging cock and scooped the helmet into her mouth like a shovel.

"Ssshit," I moaned like a bitch. Her mouth was so warm and tight.

With my right hand, I moved her hair out of the way, so I could watch her lips pull at my dick. She bobbed her head back and forth. Her neck game was always on point. Drea pulled me out of her mouth and dipped under my nut sack. My cock laid on the bridge of her nose, as she suckled on each one of my balls. Her tongue danced a little lower, teasing at the start of my ass crack.

I took two steps forward, forcing her to lean back. The back of her head now rested on the edge of the bed. Her knees, still implanted in the same spot. Her ass, sitting on her haunches. My right leg cocked up. My foot flat on the mattress. Balls dangling right above her face. I dip them into her mouth, like a tea bag.

Andrea reached up, gripped my ass with her left hand, my dick with her right, pulling me down until she was able to suck it at an angle. Damn, I love this freaky-ass bitch!

Five minutes later, I was cumming all over her face. She stuck her tongue out, catching my drip. I tapped three times on her lips with the tip of my dick, before I walked out of the bedroom, heading to go take a shower. To say I slept like a baby was an understatement.

I woke up around noon, after being doused in my sleep with ice-cold water.

"What the fuck!" I yelled, jumping out of bed, shivering.

Andrea just stood there, with an empty pot pan.

"Nigga, you got your dick sucked by that hoe Cassi last night?"

"Huh? What the fuck is you talking 'bout?"

"That bitch been on the *Gram* all morning. Talking 'bout *Don't nothing taste better than a red nigga.* Then, she gone hashtag *A.D.D.*"

I looked at her silly ass, like she was crazy.

"What the fuck does that got to do with me? My name is *A.D.* Not *A.D.D.* That shit spells *add*. Like one plus one is two. Add it up."

"Nigga, I know she sucked your dick. I smelled yo' shit, and you had a weird scent on it. Not like pussy, but like bad breath."

I started to walk away, so I could change clothes.

"Drea, mannn, miss me with that shit. I was home with you last night. Let me find out you just trynna shift blame."

She popped her neck. "Shift blame? Shift blame for what?"

"My lil' homie said he saw you hopping out of a black *Maserati* last night." She flinched. She wasn't expecting that. I knew it.

"Well, your lil' homie is a motherfucking lie. I was—"

"Look, I don't even give a fuck. I'm about to take a shower, and I don't wanna hear about that shit when I get out."

Well, imagine my surprise when I came out to find all my clothes in a pile in the garage. With this loony bitch threatening to set them on fire.

"Listen, Drea, you know them hoes be capping on the *Gram*. Why you always listening to them?"

My phone rung. I picked it up and heard the operator from the County on the line. Once I accepted, I found out *Kay* had gotten arrested for some robbery charges, but I could barely hear what he was saying. Andrea was all in the background talking loudly.

"I bet it's that bitch on the line."

"Bro, call me back," I said before hanging up. I looked at her and asked, "Why don't you call her yourself and ask her?"

"I did."

"Okay, so what she say?"

"She talking 'bout some nigga she fuck with that goes to *U of H*, got the same initials." I could tell she hated to admit that out loud.

I turned my palms up. "Okay, so what the fuck? You in here acting retarded, my nigga." I see her shoulders slump. I smell weakness, and go in for the kill.

"Look, Drea, you're a grown-ass woman. This right here, is lil' girl shit. The same clothes you finna burn, I got to go right back out there and buy. That's less money I can spend on your crazy ass."

She crossed her arms over her chest, pouting. I knew I had her.

"Now, give me the lighter fluid, babe."

She looked down, as if it was the first time seeing it. I extended my hand. She slowly handed it over. I tossed it into the corner.

Once I realized the threat was neutralized, I walked past her and went to retrieve some trash bags, filling them up to capacity. I made a promise to myself to get on *Cassie's* ass about this messy ass shit.

Twelve Months Later

Kaydon

I came back from court, exhausted. My court-appointed attorney is talking like he can beat it. So, once we submitted a motion to discover, we found out exactly what happened. Apparently, the same two white boys who came to score them pills from *Rambo aka Rah* did in fact get robbed that night. Who robbed them? *Rambo aka Rashard.* And of course, the other two niggas of my crew, *AD* and *Demon.*

Yeah, just as I had suspected. Rah and the guys led the two of them to a vaco, where they pistol-whipped and robbed them. They even went as far as confiscating their SUV. The two victims wrote statements claiming a Black guy wearing a red and white *Polo* shirt, jumping in a burnt orange *Impala,* had something to do with it.

On the contrary, I wanted nothing to do with that bullshit. But here I am. Rashard was supposed to get me a free-world lawyer, but something happened and he couldn't come through. My bond was set at three hundred thousand. A hundred and fifty bands for each. I didn't have thirty bands on deck, and my hoe-ass brother was acting funny.

So, here I was. A year in, and set for trial. I told my lawyer I didn't do it, but I know who did. He spent six months trying to convince me to snitch. That was not about to happen. Then, he asked me if the guys would sign affidavits. They said they would at first, but after consideration, we figured if I took it to trial, there was no way I could get convicted. I had *Keeda*, who was going to testify that I was at her house all night. What it came down to was pray and hope for the best.

I came back to the tank and laid it down. Five hours later, I felt someone shaking me awake.

"Kay. Kay. They calling you for visit, my nigga."

I opened my eyelids and could barely make out where I was at. Damn, I'm back in jail. I was having a good-ass dream. I shook the cobwebs off, got up, brushed my teeth, washed my face, and headed to visitation.

I'd been on the same tank, on the same floor, for a year. So, I knew almost all of the deputies. I walked to the central picket. *Ms. Flarnoy* was working.

"Can you tell me who came to see me?"

She looked at the slip, then showed it to me. My mom's and *Danielle's* name was on the slip.

A slight jolt of anger coursed through me. In the past year, Danielle came to see me maybe five times. It seemed as if she always had an excuse. Then, whenever I called, it was like she was always rushing me off the phone. I'm not a fool. I knew she was probably fucking other niggas. But damn, at least be there for me mentally.

I walked into the visit with a mug on my face. Until I saw my mother. She had the biggest smile anyone could have. My T-Lady had been coming to see me at least once a week for twelve months. Rain, sleet, or snow.

I glanced at Danielle. She was rocking an *Ed Hardy* shirt, with some black *Ed Hardy* stretch pants. With her hair and nails done, she was the baddest thing in visitation. Well, besides my momma.

"Hey, baby, how was court?"

Even though she attended most of my hearings, she still asked the same question every time.

"Hey, momma. My lawyer talking like he can beat it. I have witness statements from people that will testify I was somewhere else at the time."

I couldn't help but notice Danielle flinch at the mention of that. No doubt, she'd heard about *Keeda* from somebody. I know I didn't tell her.

"Well, that's a good thing. Just pray about it, baby. You said you didn't do anything, so the good Lord will set you free," my momma preached.

No matter how strongly she believed, I still wasn't about to put my life in someone's hands I couldn't see or touch. Especially since niggas were getting fucked by the system daily. Momma and I talked for about another three minutes, then she left to give Danielle and me some privacy.

I looked at her, disgust written all over my face.

"Wassup?"

She gave me this weak-ass smile. "Hey, Kay."

"My nigga, what you got going on? I've been locked up a year, and I can count on one hand how many times you done came up here to see a nigga. Then, when I can get through on the phone, you always trynna rush a nigga off. We don't even rock out for the whole call."

She put her head down, before looking up at me with misty eyes.

"Look, I'm sorry, Kay. This shit is just . . . It's hard for me. Them white folks talking 'bout twenty to thirty years. I don't know, I guess I'm just scared to lose you. Every time I come up here, or we talk on the phone, I'm reminded of that. I don't know if I could handle it, if it came to that."

Hearing her voice, her worries, caused me to soften my stance a little.

"D, I understand all this is new. Shit, it's new to me. But you can't just turn your back on a nigga. You say you love me, then be there for me. I know you out there fucking, but—"

"I'm not fucking nobody," she tried to convince me.

"Okay, D, whatever. If you was fucking somebody, then I can't trip about it. Just don't lose sight of a nigga. My lawyer said he can beat this shit, so I will be home soon anyway."

Danielle wiped the tears from her cheeks.

"You're right, Kay. I'm sorry I haven't been doing the things I'm supposed to. I promise, I'll do better. No matter what."

We spent the rest of the time playing catch-up. After the visit was over, I felt a little better. I had my girl back in my corner.

Six Weeks Later

"We, the jury, sentence the defendant, Kaydon Snow, to forty years in the Texas Department of Criminal Justice."

My ears won't stop ringing. My chest felt tight. I think I might be having a heart attack. Forty years . . . what the fuck!

I look to my left. My bum-ass court-appointed attorney looks dumbstruck. I have an uncontrollable urge to knock his bitch ass out. How the fuck did I get convicted, much less sentenced to forty years?

I vaguely hear my mother going off in the courtroom. I looked behind me and saw the bailiffs trying to restrain her. She was the only one that showed up to my trial.

Danielle came through during jury selection and opening statements, but hadn't been back since. Maybe it's best that she wasn't here.

I felt the bailiff grab ahold of my arm and escort me back to the holding tank.

Other inmates swarm me, asking, "How did it go? How much time did they give you?"

It's like they couldn't see I wasn't in the mood to socialize. I didn't know what to think, much less say. My life was over with. I refused to cry about it. I tried to prepare myself mentally for the journey ahead.

My court-appointed slinks towards the back to let me know about my appeal rights. I want to spit in his face, but the glass is separating us.

I make it back to the tank around five-thirty in the evening. Of course, everyone on the pod wants to know what they gave me. I tell them forty years, because I know they'll just keep asking.

I called the house and laced Danielle up. She broke down and cried over the phone. She kept asking me what she should do. I honestly don't have the answer. I didn't think I would lose. I'm actually innocent. She promised she would be there for me.

I wanted so badly to believe her, but . . .

The next three phone calls, we discussed the appeal process, visitation policies in TDCJ, and what I expect from her. We hung the phone up right before rack time.

Once I'm tucked firmly in bed, with a blanket over my head, then do I allow myself to cry.

Chapter 3

Danielle

I hung the phone up with *Kaydon* and laid back in bed. The pillow, soaked with my tears. He just got done telling me the news. Forty years! I know deep down in my heart, I won't be able to do it. I want to. I really do. But that's a long-ass time. I need to be held. I need to be loved. I don't know the first thing about being a jailhouse wife. He expects so much from me, and I know I'll disappoint him.

As I'm sitting there grieving, I decide I can't be alone for the night. I pick up my phone, scroll through my contacts, and dial a number.

"Hello?"

"What you doing tonight?"

"I ain't got shit planned. Why, wassup?"

He knows damn well why I'm calling. He just wants to hear me say it.

"I just got some bad news. Can you come over?"

I hear mumbling, as if he's conferring with someone else.

"Well, I'm with my nigga right now. We can slide though."

He leaves the proposition unspoken. Basically, if I want him to come give me that dick, his homeboy has to come also.

I could call someone else who doesn't have as much baggage, but right now, I need what he has to offer. I bite my bottom lip, then answer his proposal.

"Slide though, but make sure y'all bring me some four bars."

"How many you need?"

"At least three or four."

"I got you."

Before he hangs up, I make sure to tell him, "Don't forget the rubbers. I be letting you hit raw, but I don't know your nigga like that."

I hear a slight chuckle before he responds.

"Fa shit sho, I got you, Dee. We on the way."

Forty-five minutes later, *Pusha* walks through the door with his homeboy *Dank* right behind him. Since we all know why we're here, there's no need for false pretenses or formalities. I know they got an eyeful when they saw I was in nothing but a black lace thong with a matching bra.

"Damn, Dee, you ain't playing no games, huh?" Pusha commented, as they got comfortable, sitting down on the couch and twisting up a blunt of *Loud*.

I extend my hand out. "Where my shit at?"

He pulled a small *Advil* bottle out of his pocket and tossed it to me. I know how fucked up the pill game is, so I pop one first and wait to see what it does. After ten minutes, I feel the drug take its effect. My mouth becomes dry, but my pussy becomes wet.

As my eyelids dropped, I stared at Pusha and his homeboy Dank, trying to guess who had the bigger dick. I'd met Pusha on the Southwest one night, while I was out clubbing with my homegirl *Nikki*. Him and his *Crip* homeboys were in the club acting up. Before the night was done, we'd exchanged numbers.

To be honest, now that I was studying the both of them, I realized they resembled each other. Both were over six feet tall, two hundred plus, and dark-skinned.

"Sooo. Who's first?" I asked, with a slight slur.

Before I could blink, both dicks were out. I walked over to the couch and started with Pusha, working his Dickies and boxers off while I slowly bobbed on his sizable cock.

"Hmmm," I moaned around it, as I felt him grow to the size I'm accustomed to.

After three or four minutes of work, I moved over and did the same for Dank. I had to admit to myself, his dick tasted scrumptious. I cuffed his balls in my hands. They felt heavy and full of cum. I needed to do something about that.

While I gobbled up Dank's dick, I used my left hand to jack Pusha off. I wanted to make sure both of them were equipped to fuck my pain away.

Once I felt they were both ready, I stood up, unhooked my bra, and peeled my soggy, wet thong off. I grabbed two condoms out of the box of *Magnums* they brought and tossed them their way.

"Strap up!"

After both dicks were covered up, I directed traffic.

"Dank, lay down on the floor."

As he got in position, I rubbed my clit vigorously in a circle. I felt my nut bubbling, so I stopped to bring it back down. I want the first nut I buss to coat someone's cock.

Dank laid down, his fat-ass dick sticking straight up in the air. I straddled his lap, sinking down until his balls kissed my ass cheeks. I felt him all in my stomach. I welcomed the pain.

I leaned forward, my tits pressed into his chest. I looked back at Pusha.

"Nigga, you know what to do."

I grabbed both my booty cheeks and splayed them open, giving him unobstructed access to my backdoor. I heard him spit, then felt it land and drip down the crack of my ass. He worked two fingers into my shit hole to loosen me up. I moaned in anticipation. Dank's dick twitched inside my cunt. He was revving up to go.

I bit my lip as I felt Pusha's tip break through my barrier. A sharp pinch, then the burning sensation as his dickhead bore through my anal cavity. After three short strokes, he was now also balls deep.

I've never felt so full in my life. The mixture of pain and pleasure was so exquisite.

Slowly, they began to rock back and forth, building up rhythm. My coochie was wet as hell, but so was my booty hole.

"Oh fuck. Oh fuck. Damn, this shit feels soooo good," I groaned, as they began to pound into me.

The friction created electric currents that lit my clit up like a light bulb. In no time at all, I felt my nut come crashing down like an avalanche.

"Oh Gawd. Oh Gawd, I'm finna cum. Ssshit, I'm cummminnggg!"

My whole body convulsed. I held on for dear life as they fucked me down through not one, but two orgasms. Back to back. They didn't spare me at all, and I didn't want them to.

Three hours later, and six condoms lighter, the two walked out of my apartment while I laid on the floor. Covered in sweat and cum. My legs spread wide. My asshole and pussy busted open.

I was so exhausted, I couldn't even get up to go lock the door behind them.

I fell asleep right there on my living room floor. *Stress free.*

Rashard

"Say, my nigga, you heard how much time they said *Kay* got?" *Demon* asked, as we rode down *Woodforest Blvd.*

"Yeah, his T-Lady said they gave him forty years." Demon stared out the window for a while before he said anything. I can tell something was eating at him. Even though we were all close, *Kaydon* is the one that stepped up to help him against the *Crips*. Once Kay vouched for him, the rest of us were automatic.

"Blood, we should've done something to help him," he finally said.

"What could we have done? You think we should've turned ourselves in?"

Just hearing me say it out loud sounded so ridiculous.

"Bro, I don't know. We could've all come together and gotten him a lawyer or something. Ain't no way he should've lost that trial. I just feel like a bitch-ass nigga. Bro ain't have shit to do with that. He took the lick, and he could've ratted us out, but he kept it G. I just think we could've done more to help."

I can tell Demon is hurt about Kay getting all that time.

"To be honest," I tell him, "I didn't think bro would get found guilty. I mean, damn, he ain't do shit."

I'm still trying to wrap my head around the fact that twelve people found him guilty, and he was forty miles away. That goes to show you the system is severely broken.

Demon gets quiet. We both are lost in our thoughts when I turn into *Danielle's* apartments.

I parked, then turned towards him. "Look, I'm 'bout to give *D* some money for bro. I'll be right back."

"Wait, hold up." Demon goes into his pocket and pulls out a hundred-dollar bill. "I know it ain't much, but here. Tell her to tell bro I said wassup, and much love."

I grabbed the money, then hopped out. When I knocked on Danielle's door, it doesn't take her long to answer. She was rocking a *Victoria's Secret PINK* robe. Underneath, a matching set of purple bra and panties. One thing about Danielle—when she's home, she barely wears any clothes.

Stepping in, I give her a hug, cuffing her ass cheeks in the process. Her booty feels soft and fluffy. My dick instantly rocks up, poking her in the stomach. She moaned into my mouth.

"Are you a'ight?" I asked, as we separated.

"Yeah, I'm good. *Kay* was my first love. Shit, he's my only love. I don't know what to do without him," she admitted.

"Well, you know I'll be here for you if you need anything. Matter fact . . . ." I pulled out the hundred Demon gave me and added another hundred to it. "Here, this for you. I know it ain't much, but I'll pull back up during the week and drop off something else. I know you'll probably need a lil help with the bills from time to time."

She nodded in appreciation. "Thank you so much, *Rah*." Then, she bit her bottom lip.

"You know what . . . ." Danielle grabbed my hand and led me into the bedroom. She had me sit on the bed as she kneeled between my thighs and pulled out my dick to give me a thank-you blow job.

Ten minutes later, I tilted my head back and growled, "Fuck. I'm finna nut."

My warm seed fills her mouth. She doesn't waste a drop. I watch her throat muscles work my cum down her trachea. Danielle smacked her lips before staring into my eyes and smiling.

She tucks me back in. I stood up, gave her a hug, and headed out of the apartment.

Once I get back to the car, Demon is staring out the passenger window, deep in thought.

"You trynna smoke one?" I offer up.

He frowned his face up. "Naw, I'm good, my nigga."

I detect a hint of anger, but don't acknowledge it.

After ten minutes of silence, he asked me to drop him off at his twin sister *Debra's* house.

"I thought we was gon' hit the park up?" I asked.

"Naw, I'm good. I gotta help my sister with something," he claimed.

"A'ight. Fuck it," I mumbled under my breath, as I hit the U-turn, headed back the other way to drop his sour ass off.

Demon

Two minutes after the homie *Rah* went into the spot, I realized I had some money in my sock. I wanted to send the homie *Kay* more than just a yard. I pulled my phone out and dialed Rah's number. I heard his phone start going off, and realized he left it in the car.

Fuck!

I jumped out the whip and made my way to the apartment. I knocked, but the door crept open. I pushed through and realized the living room was empty. I walked in and checked the kitchen. Also empty. I made my way through the hallway and heard moaning and what sounds like loud sucking and slurping.

A sick sense forms in the pit of my stomach.

The bedroom door is closed, but not completely. I pushed it open, slowly. What I saw fucked me up. Rah was on the bed, with his head tilted back. The big homie's girl was on her knees, sucking the skin off his dick.

I felt I should've said something. Both of them were out of line. But as I go to speak, my voice catches in my throat.

I stand there stuck, watching as she spears her head into his lap so fast, that her ass cheeks jiggled from the velocity. My dick began to rise.

I turned around and headed back outside. I couldn't look at Rah the same after seeing what I saw. I understand, hoes gon' be hoes, but the homie just bit a bullet for us. The least we could do is have respect and loyalty towards what's his.

I hit my twin sister *Debra* up, to see if I could head over to her crib. She told me yes, so I waited on Rah to get done.

Fifteen minutes later, he comes back to the car. I debate on what I should do. Should I confront him? Should I write *Kay* and expose him? But then again, the homie's going through a lot right now, and the last thing I want to do is add to that.

"Fuck it, Imma just keep my mouth shut," I mumbled to myself, as Rah opens the door to get in.

At the end of the day, it's none of my business.

Rah tried to hold a conversation with me, but I'm not feeling dude. We were supposed to hit the park and play ball, but now I just need some space. I told him to just drop me off at my sister's.

When we pulled up, I hopped out and left his outstretched hand hanging. Left him to wonder why I refused to shake it.

Kaydon

I walked into my cell, plugged my hot pot in, and grabbed the necessary items for my meal. Instead of leaving me on a transfer facility, they sent me straight to Hughes Unit, central Texas.

My nigga A-1 had done time over there, so I knew a little bit about how they were rocking. When I pulled up, I noticed they had niggas with titties walking around. That shit fucked me up. I ended up linking in with some niggas from the city. Turns out, Hughes was also known for a lot of homosexual activity.

As I let the water heat up in the pot, I grabbed my tablet and noticed I have a couple new e-messages. They were both from my brother's wife, Claudia. I was surprised to see she had even hooked her account up. Since I'd been gone, my momma was the only one who had written me. I opened the message and noticed I also have some pictures attached. I decided to read the letter first.

Dear Kay Kay

I hope you don't mind me calling you that. I heard that was your family nickname when you were little. I know you're probably surprised to see me writing. Well, don't be. I consider us family and I don't abandon family. I know you're upset because your brother Harrell didn't help you out. You have the right to be. I know he could be extreme sometimes. I'm helping him work on that. I talked to Lavella. She told me what went down at your trial, and how they railroaded you. As you may not know, I work at a law firm as a secretary. I plan on speaking to a few attorneys, to see if it's anything I can do. Don't get your hopes up just yet though. I also sent some pictures, and I'll send more soon. Take care of yourself.

Big Sis

I downloaded the pics from the first message and the other two from the second. There were four in total. One, she was in her work clothes. Business skirt and blouse. Two of them, she was at home cooking in the kitchen. The last one was of her at the beach in Galveston. She had on a red, two-piece bikini. I couldn't help but to zoom in on her most sacred parts. *Lawd, have mercy!*

I could clearly see her sex lips, through the thin, wet material. And man, her pussy was fat as hell. Claudia was definitely a bad bitch. Born in Columbia, she came to America when she was just a kid, so her English was flawless.

Five foot five, light complexion, melon sized tits, slim waist and a booty like Cardi B. Not to mention, a pair of luscious pink lips. By the looks of it, her other lips might be just the same. I must have stared at the picture for an hour straight. Her nipples were poking through the bikini top. Claudia definitely had it going on. I read the letter again. *I wonder if she'll be able to help?* I sure hoped so. I wasn't going to get my hopes up though. I decided to write her back, asap.

Hey Claudia,

Thanks for the letter and pics. I really enjoyed them. I'm not sweating my bro; it is what it is. It's just messed up. You're willing to be there more for me than he is. I hope you can find one of those lawyers up there to help me out. And yes, I did get railroaded, but I can't talk about my case on this device. I'll put you on my list. Since you and bro are married, it'll be contact. Oh, and I don't mind you calling me Kay Kay. Most people just say Kay now, but I'm cool with whatever. I've been hitting the law library every day, as well as working out. Gotta keep the body and mind in shape. Once again, thanks for the pics. I didn't know you had it like that. DAMN! LOL. Talk to you soon.

Kay Kay

I sent the message off with a smile. As soon as my food was done cooking, my celly Hector came in on the in-and-out. He was a five foot, eight inch, dark-skin Mexican from Laredo, who was doing ten years, non-agg, for a half a brick of coke. He told me he worked for the Cartel, but shit, it seemed like every Mexican in the pen claimed the same thing.

We'd been cellies since I pulled up on the unit.

"Aye, celly, you have no queso?"

Sometimes, it took me a while to try and process what he was trying to say.

"You need some cheese?" I asked.

He nodded emphatically. I reached into my locker and handed him the last of my squeeze cheese. He spread it over a *lockup* burrito he made while he was in the dayroom.

We ate in silence. Once we were done, the bowls cleaned and put away, he asked, "You want see mi pics?"

I shrugged my shoulders. "Sure, why not?"

He grabbed his tablet off his bunk and clicked into his picture gallery. What I saw blew my mind. He had pictures of him and his Cartel buddies. They're hopping out of big-ass pickup trucks, draped in gold and diamonds. It seemed as if he had a bad bitch on his arm in every picture. He showed me pictures of a couple eighteen-wheelers he owned, as well as a few homes. One of them looked like a ranch in Mexico.

It took me an hour to look through all his pictures.

I began to feel self-conscious. I had a total of ten pics on my tablet. Six from my mom, and the four I just got from Claudia. Luckily, he doesn't ask to look at mine.

"Celly, when you get out?"

"Shit, I got forty years. But my homegirl said she might be able to find me a lawyer."

He nodded, as if he understood completely.

"You hustle, no?"

"Hell yeah I hustle. That's all I know. I'm not a jack boy. This robbery charge is bogus as hell," I say, vehemently.

Hector studied me for a brief moment. "You get out, I uhh . . . how you say — put you on?"

I almost laugh. "So, what you saying? You wanna be my plug?"

He nodded emphatically.

"Si. Si."

"Man, I hope you're for real. I do need a plug."

"No bullshit. My word," he assured me.

We spent a half an hour talking 'bout dope prices and different ways to handle coke, delivery, and building a team. On the next in-and-out, I leave the cell to give him some cell time.

As I hit the dayroom, I looked around. All I saw was overgrown kids. Slap boxing, rapping, high as hell off K2. I catch a seat, then check my phone account. I still have only one number on there. My mom's.

I still can't believe none of my niggas, or Danielle, has the phone set up. A part of me starts to tell myself, maybe I should have gave them niggas up. But I quickly dispelled that. I kept it real, 'cause I'm a real nigga. I didn't have a choice.

Still, that shit hurts like hell, knowing the ones you've sacrificed your life for can't even set up the free phone account.

I say *fuck it*, then call my T-Lady.

"Hello?"

"Hey, momma."

"Hey, boo, wassup?"

"Nothing. In the dayroom, watching *SportsCenter*. What you got going on?"

"Oh, nothing. Just left Linda's house. Oh, that reminds me, Rashard asked about you."

My face instantly frowns up. "I don't see why he's asking you about me, when he could set the phone up and ask me himself."

"I know, baby. I told him how to set it up last week, so I don't know what his deal is."

"I'm not even tripping 'bout that no more. What Danielle got going on?"

"Kaydon, I don't see that girl anymore. She don't even call to check up on me, like she used to do when you was in the county. You know how them girls are."

I can't do nothing but grunt in reply.

That bitch ain't even last six months.

I promised myself right then and there, if I ever get a chance to escape this hellhole, I was going to make everybody pay. If it wasn't my momma, fuck them.

Her and I rode for a few more minutes, but she said she needed to get ready. She and Ms. Linda were going out.

"Okay, momma, tell Ms. Linda I said wassup."

"You know I will."

After I got off the phone with my T-Lady, I sat and stared at the wall, with a mug on my face.

I think the worst feeling in the world is to give up everything for someone, just to find out they don't give a fuck about you.

Chapter 4

AD

Life is good. I just left the dice game, where I hit for six bands. See, I'm not the type of nigga that shoots dice until he's broke. If I see I'm up, and my shot ain't on, then I'm out.

I decided to slide up to Andrea's job real quick. See if I can get some head in the parking lot. She worked at a department store on Wallisville and the Beltway, and had been working there for the last four years.

When I pulled up, I made sure I parked on the side, near a street called Blackrock. I knew that was a virtual blind spot for the cameras. Only reason I knew is 'cause Drea's friends with some lame-ass nigga in security, named David.

Anyway, I walked in and headed straight to the Electronics section. I looked for her, but didn't see her anywhere. I asked her coworker, some white chick with the name *Kelsey* printed on her name tag, "Say, do you know where Andrea is?"

Kelsey looked at me, and I could tell she was trying to decide if she should divulge her coworker/friend's whereabouts.

"That's my baby momma," I assured her.

"Oh. Umm, she went on break."

"Break? When did she go on break?" I asked, suspiciously.

She looked at her *G-Shock*. "Um, like five minutes ago."

Five minutes? I know I didn't see her walk past me when I came in.

"Do y'all have a break room, or somewhere y'all go chill at on break?"

"Well, some people go to the burger stand across the street."

Something about the way she kept fidgeting led me to believe she was lying through her teeth. Still, I thanked her and headed back to the front of the store.

Once I stepped outside, I pulled my phone out and dialed Drea's number. It rang four times, then went to voicemail. So, I text: *Where you at?*

Seven minutes go by, no reply. I tried to call again. No response. Now, I'm getting pissed. This bitch is always playing these types of reindeer games.

I check the time on my *Hub lot*. 4:15 p.m. I shoot over to the burger spot across the street. She isn't there either. I debate whether I should head home, but something tells me to head back to her job. I park my car and wait it out.

Forty-five minutes later, I feel my phone vibrate. I check and see I have a text message. I see the bitch finally decided to text back.

Andrea: *I'm at work, where u at?*

Instead of replying, I hopped out of my car and stormed inside. I have to be careful. The way I'm feeling, I'll fuck around and do some stupid shit, and end up on *Channel 12* news.

As soon as I got to her station, I could tell she was nervous about something. I didn't waste any time with pleasantries.

"Bitch. Where the fuck have you been?"

She has the nerve to look at me as if I'm the slowest human being on Earth.

"I've been at work, AD. Duh."

I wanted to snatch her ass up by her throat for the blatant disrespect. I grit my teeth and tried my best to control my anger.

"Say, Drea, don't play with me. I just came through looking for your ass. You wasn't here."

She frowned her face up, as if I was bothering her.

"Boy, I was in the restroom taking a shit. Damn, what the fuck is a bitch gonna do at work? Gone on with all that extra shit, nigga."

I snapped, reached out and grabbed her by the face, squeezing the life out of her jawline.

"Bitch, you think it's a game? I'll rewire your whole fucking jaw," I growl through clenched teeth.

"Say, man, you need to leave." I hear a male voice.

I turned to see some six-foot, three-inch, bald-headed nigga standing behind me. He had on a T-shirt and jeans, but I could tell he was with security. I released my grip on her face, turned so that I could face the nigga.

I heard Andrea say, "It's alright, David. This my baby daddy. He was just leaving."

At the mention of my title, I detected a smirk, but it disappeared quick as it came. We stared each other down, for what seemed like forever. Each of us unwilling to falter.

My adrenaline was up. My heart, booming in my chest. I gave a fuck that he had me by six inches and close to thirty-five pounds. The way I was feeling, I needed to put my hands on somebody.

"AD?" I heard a familiar female voice.

I turned around to catch Ms. Linda and Ms. Lavella looking at me as if I was a vicious pit bull that somehow made it out of the yard.

"Boy, what you doing in here?"

My anger instantly dissipated.

I took two breaths to calm my nerves before I responded. A half smile crept upon my face.

"Umm. Nothing really, Ms. Linda. I just came up here to holla at Andrea. I'm 'bout to head out though."

I take a look at how both of them are dressed. Each has a short-ass skirt. Their thick, smooth thighs on full display.

Ms. Linda, Rah's momma, was a bad old-school bitch. She had one of those big ole stripper booties. I know she was a fool back in her day. But it was something about Kay's momma, Ms. Lavella, that did something to me. Yellow bone, with a forty-inch ass and a pair of succulent double-D's.

I remember being in the tenth grade. I'd gone over to the homie's house and caught his momma coming out of the bathroom in her bra and panties. I still have dreams about her coochie eating up the crotch of her thong like a lioness does a gazelle on the plain lands.

I went right in the same bathroom, jacked my dick until I came not once, but twice.

"Where y'all headed?" I wanted to be nosey.

"Well, if you must know, they have a trail ride coming through Pleasantville later today. We 'bout to go have us a little cowgirl fun," Linda said.

I can only imagine what type of fun they had in mind. I knew a couple big homies about their age, who said they knew them when they were younger. Word on the street: they were both *Boss Freaks*.

I could see Ms. Lavella's nipples were now hard. Wonder what she was thinking.

I had to get somewhere before I embarrassed myself.

"Well, y'all ladies don't have too much fun," I called out, as I began to leave.

As an afterthought, I turned around. "Ms. Lavella, how is Kaydon doing?"

She gave a slight frown but said, "He's alright. He wishes y'all would write and send him some money though."

"Tell him I got him. Soon as I get some bread, I'll shoot some his way."

Yeah, I'd just hit for six bands on the dice, but I had plans for that doh. Once I flipped it a couple times, I'd shoot Kay a couple hundred or something.

After saying my goodbyes, I head out to the parking lot and back to my car. I'm still pissed at the way Drea tried to play me.

I checked my phone and saw I had a message from her:

Andrea: *You tripping for nothing, babe. U act like I'm in a nigga face or something. U C I'm at work.*

Yeah, whatever. I don't even bother to reply.

I called Cassi up, to see what she had on her menu.

Of course nothing. I head her way to feed her this dick.

Andrea

I'm tapping my feet, anxious for my break to get here. I checked my watch again.

"Where the fuck is she at?" I mumbled to myself.

My coworker Kelsey went on break, but was supposed to have been back by now. I checked my watch for the tenth time in the last thirty seconds. Didn't she know I had some important shit to do?

Finally, I saw her pale, pink ass bend the corner.

"My bad, girl. I was arguing with my dude," she explained, but I was only half listening.

I clocked my register out and grabbed my purse. Instead of heading out the front door, I slide to the back, where the security station is located.

As soon as I entered David's office, we wasted no time. He's seated in an office chair, his legs wide open. I locked the door behind me and dropped to my knees in front of him. My mouth salivates at the promise of that hard, chocolate cock I'm about to taste.

I unzipped his jeans and roughly pulled them down past his knees. His dick was already up, but leaning over to the side. I guess it needed some straightening.

I grabbed his shaft with my right hand, balls with my left. His nuts felt hot and heavy. I leaned in and sniffed. He had a slight musk, but when I licked his dickhead, I tasted Zest soap. My craving increased. I opened wide and took him all in.

"Oh my Jesus, girl. Damn, Andrea."

I love the power I have on a man when I'm on my knees and his dick is in my mouth.

My lips locked around his shaft as I pulled him in and out of my jaws. I worked him slow at first, but he began to pop his hips, eager for more. He yearned to fuck my throat like he does my pussy or my booty hole.

I allow him a few minutes, but I need to feel his heavy-duty cock slamming into my twat.

I pulled back and allowed his dick to flop out of my mouth, slick with my spit. I stood up and shimmed out of my work khakis. By now, he has discarded his jeans, and he's in nothing but a T-shirt and socks, but he kept his shoes on—for the extra grip.

He forced me to turn around before yanking my panties down to my knees. I felt him cuff on my coochie, sliding his middle finger up and down my slit. He doesn't have to tell me I'm wet—I could feel it running down my inner thigh.

Shit, I can smell how wet I am. The same way you can smell fresh rain when it's coming.

My palms are flat against the wall to brace myself.

SMACK! My right cheek stings as his heavy hand slapped it silly. I'm pushed forward even further. Now, my face is flush against the cold concrete.

I felt the heat from his cock before I felt the penetration. My sex lips opened up to receive him. Then *bam!* He slammed his gun into my holster.

I bit down on my bottom lip as he began to thrust back and forth. My booty cheeks clapped and cheered as he crashed into them. Over and over.

My nipples were so hard, they hurt. I find the strength to reach under my shirt and flip them out of the confines of my bra.

With my face against the wall, my left hand tweaking my nipples, it felt like my bladder was about to buss.

David is unrelenting. I yelled for him to "Hold up. Hold up. Hold up," but he doesn't quit, and before I knew it, I was cumming in waves.

"Aww fuck, I'm cumming, I'm cumming," I screamed.

He pulled back so he could watch the waterworks. I squirt cum all over the office tiles, sodding my panties in the process.

The nasty-ass freak squats down and lapped at my juices from the back. Each time his tongue touched my clit, I shivered and shook.

I looked down at my ruined pair of drawers and had no choice but to step out of them.

David turned me around and pulled me towards him as he sat back down on his office chair. I reached back, grabbed his dick, and eased down until he filled me up to the brim.

"Sssshit. Damn boy, this dick feels *soooo* good," I moaned as I began to rock my hips in a circular motion.

You could literally hear his cock stirring in my pot.

Squish—squish. Squish—squish.

I leaned forward and made that ass bounce in his lap like a '64 Impala.

Clap—clap—clap—clap.

"Oh fuck, Drea. Damn, girl. Get that dick. Make that muthafucka spit up," he urged.

I do just that. My walls snapped at his cock, pulling his cum from the depths of his ballsack.

The cool air tickles my puckered asshole, so I know he has a courtside view of my round, brown booty hole.

"Put your finger in it," I called out.

He licked his thumb, then worked it into my backdoor. My walls clamped down even more around his rod, causing him to howl out.

"Aww fuck! Here it cummmmsss, Drea. Here it cummmsss. Come get this shit, girl, come get it."

I hopped off, turned around, and swallowed his dick whole.

"Ahh ssshit!" he hissed, as his gun went off into my mouth.

Liquid pellets sprayed the back of my throat. I swallow without so much as a blink. He shivered and shook as I continued to suck and pull.

Finally, it's too much. He taps me on the shoulder, letting me know he's had enough.

I pull him out with a *pop* and check my watch.

"We still have twenty minutes," I tell him. "You know the deal."

Him and I have an agreement—if I spend my lunch hour in his office, then I need an hour worth of dick. And if he taps out, I get the meat substitute: tongue.

I laid back on his desk. Legs wide, with my knees touching my chest. I looked down at my coochie. My lips are engorged, heavy-looking.

I watched as he spread them apart while peeling the hood back on my clit. His tongue slithers across the tip. I shivered and jerked.

Hallelujah!

He spits on my button and rubs it with his thumb. I collapsed into a mini seizure, balling my fists up, fighting the urge to close my legs around his head.

David clamps on to my nub and begins to suck on it like a straw in a strawberry slushie.

My legs grip the sides of his head as my orgasm comes tumbling over a cliff.

"Huh. Huh. Huh. Huh." I pant, trying to stave it off.

Three fingers slide into my box. I hear my cunt making all types of disgusting noises. I couldn't hold out any longer.

"Oh my Gawd, I'm finna cum. Lawrd have mercy, I'm cummmmminnnggg!" I yell out as I explode all over his face.

David doesn't miss a beat—catching and slurping up everything I threw at him.

Twenty minutes later, he ceases the smacking and finally comes up for air.

My body's still tingling. My heart, beating down my chest cavity.

We both laughed when we realized we only had five minutes to spare. I hurry up and get dressed, throw my saturated thong in my back pocket, and head back to my work station.

As soon as I get back, Kelsey has a worried look on her face. My afterglow immediately began to dim.

"What's wrong?" I asked.

"Andrea, your baby daddy was just up here."

"What? Where?"

I instinctively began to look around. The last thing I needed was this nigga to be acting a fool at my job.

Kelsey takes note of my anxiety.

"He's gone. He asked me where you were. I told him you went on break. Then, he asked me where do we go when we're on break. I said the burger spot across the street. He left after that."

I exhale a breath of relief.

"Girl, I owe you one."

I didn't know if she knew I was fucking David on the job, but I'm glad she was game enough to cover for me. I'm definitely gonna have to start fucking with her on some G shit.

What made AD come up here? I wondered. He usually always lets me know he's on the way.

I pulled out my phone and realized I had it on *DND* (*Do Not Disturb*). I shook my head and mumbled to myself.

"This nigga 'bout to be all in my ass."

His text came in almost an hour ago. I texted back:

I'm at work. Where R U?

I waited on his reply.

Not even two minutes later, I saw his face—and he was not happy.

Of course, the first thing he does is put his hands on me. I'm thinking like, *I'm 'bout to lose my job.* I've already lost custody of our son.

Well, my momma has him.

A while back, AD had gotten into some legal trouble.

Fat story slim, C.P.S. felt because I wouldn't stop dealing with him, I was an unfit mother. *Whatever!*

I could tell the nigga was pissed the fuck off. The crazy thing was, while he had me by the face, the only thing I was thinking was, *I hope he don't smell that nigga's dick and cum on my breath.*

Just when I'm thinking he's about to go in my mouth, I hear David come to the rescue. AD reluctantly lets me go, and they have a face-off.

Now, don't get me wrong, David's a big dude, but my baby daddy AD is a savage. I know for a fact he doesn't give a fuck about the size advantage his opponent has on him.

Like any other project or hood chick, that gangsta shit turns me on.

But I'm not trying to lose my job, so I tried to diffuse the situation.

Luckily, Ms. Linda and Ms. Lavella show up. That seemed to do the trick, and AD ended up leaving.

"Are you alright?" David asked, but I'm not in the mood to talk.

"Yeah, I'm cool. It's nothing."

He looked as if he wanted to press about it, but my facial expression alerted him this was not the time.

He walked off and headed to the bathroom—most likely to wash his nuts. Lord knows, he doesn't want to smell like pussy all day.

"Girl, your dude is crazy as hell," Kelsey stated.

I almost forgot she was even there.

"Yeah. Well, I'm not no saint either."

"I bet. Shit, my dude be trying to handle me too. One of these days, Imma pick something up and buss him right in his shit," Kelsey claimed.

I laughed at her, trying to sound hood.

"No offense, Kelsey, but I think a Black dude's ass whooping is worse than a white dude's ass whooping any day," I tell her.

"Huh? Girl, I don't mess with no white boy."

I turned towards her.

"What? You seem so—"

"White?"

"Well, I was gonna say proper, but . . ."

"Hold on, let me show you."

She grabbed her phone and scrolled through her picture gallery. Even though she's swiping fast, I still catch a few dick pics and wondered if they were of her man.

"Here."

She shows me a picture of a fine-ass caramel brother, with brown eyes and muscles on top of muscles.

Even though I'd just gotten fucked into the ground, I still feel my clit jump for joy.

"Where's he from?" I inquire.

"Victoria, Texas. He's been in Houston for some years though."

I don't want to set off any alarms, so I look away, as if I've lost interest.

Yeah, I will definitely have to start fucking with her a little more. I know for a fact her lil blond pussy can't tame no Black snake like it needs to be tamed.

Chapter 5

Rashard

"A'ight. So remember, it will be two niggas in the spot, and a female in the back. We ain't gotta worry 'bout the bitch. She's one of my little side pieces, named Jocelyne. She gone lure her baby daddy to the room and text me when she has him busy. So, all we gotta do is zip tie the nigga Dirty Red, then we push up in the room and tie both them up."

I stare Demon in the eyes as I talk. He's on go!

"That's a bet. So, it's a brick and twenty-five bands in that bitch? What 'bout the sticks?" he legitimately asked.

"She says he has a mini Draco he keeps under the couch cushion. Plus, he's got a Glock 33 and a Taurus .45 he keeps in the room with him. We ain't gotta worry 'bout that though—Jocelyne left the patio door open, so we don't have to pull no kick door. Once we snatch Dirty Red up, we're good. That nigga Spider gon' be knee deep in some pussy. He won't even get a chance to reach for his shit."

Demon nodded, to assure me he saw no flaws in my plan. I passed him the blunt of kush to calm his nerves a little. Even though we've kicked in a bunch of trap spots, you always get those jitters.

Dressed in a long-sleeve black shirt to cover up our tattoos, black sweats, and a black ski mask we wore like beanies, Demon and me cruised down MLK, headed to Yellowstone.

The nigga we're about to peel is a cat by the name of Spider. Spider had a lil name for himself on the Southside. His plug was his Mexican baby momma's brother. According to Jocelyne, Spider was a pussy-ass nigga with a live connect. Same as ninety percent of these so-called boss niggas out here.

We pulled up in a Toyota Camry I rented from a smoker named Sandy. All it cost was five dime rocks and ten grams of K2. I parked behind the rec center, grabbed my AK pistol, and stuffed it inside my black backpack.

To be honest, we didn't come to lay these niggas down. The way I saw it, if we hit them and they don't know who we are, then we could always hit them again.

Demon grabbed his Glock 21, with the thirty-round clip sticking out the ass end like a roach egg. After snatching up two extra clips and sliding them in his pocket, we hopped out of the car and made our way to the street behind Spider's trap house.

I look at my *G-Shock*. It's 1:30 in the morning. The streets were eerily quiet. All we hear is footsteps and our heavy breathing. A small sheen of sweat is already forming on my forehead due to the humidity.

I checked my watch again, as if time could move any faster.

"What's taking the bitch so long?" I murmur to myself.

Demon overheard me. He shrugged his shoulders and shook his head. Then he looked at me and asked, "Do you think we can trust her?"

By *her*, he meant Jocelyne.

"Hell yeah. Jocelyne's been my bitch since we were nineteen. She even stole six bands from her momma's bank account once, to get me a nine-pack when I came home from doing nine months in the county."

Jocelyne is one of those chicks that doesn't realize she's a bad bitch. She used to get teased a lot in junior high and never realized she'd outgrown that awkward, preteen stage.

And since I'm one of *those guys*, she would bend over backwards to make me happy.

Demon and I walked along the side of the house that sat directly behind Spider's trap. After hopping the fence into that yard, we jumped the fence into Spider's backyard. The patio door was around fifteen feet away.

I checked my watch again. 1:50.

"Come on, come on."

I tap my feet and my anxiety kicks into overdrive.

My phone began to vibrate. I checked the text message and smiled.

Chow Time!

I gave Demon the nod, then pulled my handheld chopstick out of the backpack. I zip it back shut, throw it over my shoulder, and pull my ski mask over my face.

We made it to the patio door and crouched down. With a gloved left hand, I slowly slid the glass door open and listened. The TV was on—it sounded like reruns of *Family Matters*.

I bit down on my bottom lip and pushed the door open wide enough for us to crawl through. I crawl in first and immediately spring to my feet, gun in hand.

I expected Dirty Red to be watching TV, but instead, he's missing.

As soon as Demon crawled in and popped up, I motioned for him to keep quiet.

I take notice of the décor. Leather couches. Fifty-two-inch flat screen on the wall. It didn't have the feel of a trap house. After securing the kitchen, we enter the living room.

Demon immediately flipped over the couch cushion and found the mini Draco. He tossed it to me and I slid it into the backpack.

I point toward the hallway that leads to the bedroom. He understood, and we made our way.

As we bend the corner, we catch the nigga Dirty Red with his ear to the bedroom door, listening to Spider and Jocelyne fucking. This clown had his pants down to his ankles, dick in his hand, jacking off.

It took everything in me not to laugh. Demon was looking at me with wide eyes, clearly surprised as I was.

We crept up on him slowly. He was so locked into what was going on behind the door, he never noticed us—until the barrel of the stick was pressed against his head.

"Nigga, don't move or say shit. If you do, on my momma, your brains gon' be all over that door."

Dirty Red threw his hands up.

Good.

"Now walk away from the door and head back into the living room."

I debate whether or not to make him pull up his pants, 'cause a nigga ain't trynna see no other nigga's dick. But then I thought about it—it might make it harder for him to run.

We watched as he waddled back toward the living room.

As soon as we saw the couches and TV, Demon whacked him across the back of the head with the pistol.

Thwack!

He fell into the couch, groaning in agony.

I quickly pressed down on him with the barrel of the AK.

"Nigga, you bet not say shit. On Jesus Christ, Imma smoke you in this hoe."

Dirty Red began to shiver. He felt the Grim Reaper breathing down the back of his neck. He looked up. All he saw was ski masks and big guns.

I slipped the backpack off, unzipped it, and pulled out the zip ties. I tossed them to Demon, who went about tying Dirty Red up—hands and feet.

Blood poured from the gash in his head. I grabbed the duct tape and taped his mouth shut.

Once he was subdued, we made our way to the bedroom.

As we get close, we hear the sounds of sex. Skin slapping. Moans and groans.

A little part of me is fucked up this weenie-ass nigga is putting dick all up in *my* bitch. Fuck the fact they have a kid together.

I twist the doorknob and push it open.

Spider's on his knees with his back toward us, hitting Jocelyne from the back.

The scent of her pussy and their sweat permeated the room.

Squish — squish — squish — squish!

She moans out as his balls tap at her clit like two big pendulums.

"Oh shit. Oh shit. Baby, you finna make this pussy cum," Jocelyne cried out.

With three long strides, I reach them. With all the strength I could muster, I cocked back and—

Thwack!

Spider tumbles over to his left, falling off the bed. His head goes through the thin-ass sheetrock.

Jocelyne immediately turned around and screamed. I slapped her hard across her face.

"Bitch, shut the fuck up before a nigga blow your wig off!" I say, with menace.

She takes her cue, shuts up, and just sits there on the bed. With her back against the headboard, knees up and her legs splayed open, we get a good look at her coochie.

Her sex lips are still swollen and slick. The mouth of her cunt, dilated from the dick she just got done taking.

My cock began to twitch.

I held the gun on her while Demon zip tied Spider's hands and feet. Then he stands up, about to do the same thing to Jocelyne. I stopped him and whispered in his ear.

He nodded in understanding, then zip tied her hands only.

After she's secured, I help him drag Spider into the living room. We placed him next to Dirty Red. Both are leaking blood everywhere, from the wounds in their skulls.

Hopefully, this would be the only blood that needs to be spilled.

"Check this out—we just came for two things. The money and the dope. Where is it?"

Of course, I already know where everything is. But I can't go straight to it. If I did, they'd know Jocelyne set them up. So I have to make them tell me themselves.

"My nigga, I don't know what they told you, but I don't sell no dope, homie," Spider tried to sell me that bullshit.

Thwack!

"Agghh! Fuuccck!" he screamed, as Demon smacked him in the mouth with the butt of the gun.

Pieces of broken teeth skip across the bloody carpet.

"You know what?" I say, as if I suddenly had a bright idea. "I'll see if your bitch will tell me. If not, I'll smoke her ass first. That is, unless you keep it a stack and just tell me where it's at."

He looks up at me defiantly.

"Have it your way," I say, as I make my way back to the bedroom.

As I walk in, I take my ski mask off. Jocelyne's sitting there, as if she doesn't have a care in the world. As soon as her eyes landed on me, her face lit up. Then, a frown.

"Nigga. You ain't have to hit a bitch that hard."

I look at her lip. It's swollen and red.

"My bad, baby girl. I had to make it believable. I told him I'd be back here roughing you up. So, I want you to put on a show."

She displayed a devilish smile.

"I can do that," she purred, knowing my intentions.

"Yeah? Well, can you do it with your hands tied and . . ."

I reached inside my sweats and pulled my dick out,

". . . your mouth full."

I walked towards the bed. She reached for my piece. With her hands zip tied together, Jocelyne gripped my cock and smeared the tip against her swollen and bruised lip.

She took her tongue and licked around my crown before stuffing me into her mouth.

I trembled with pleasure, looking down and watching as my shaft glides between her lips. Each time it emerged, it was slick and shiny.

Her left hand found my nut sack.

"Ooh *ssshit!*" I hissed, before she pulled me out of her mouth.

"Oh my God! Please! I don't know anything about any drugs or money!" she screamed for Spider's benefit, before stuffing me back in.

I weaved my fingers through her weave and palmed the back of her skull.

Five foot five inches, a hundred and forty-two pounds, banana-red skin tone, and an ass like *delicious*. Jocelyne, by all accounts, was a bad bitch. Her pussy always stayed juicy. Her head game was phenomenal.

My hips jerked as I began to fuck her throat—just like Spider was doing her box earlier when we walked in.

Just picturing him digging her out had me furious as hell. I plant my feet and began to grudge-fuck her face. My dickhead punching through her esophagus.

Her eyes started to tear up.

I pulled back and she gasped for air.

"Please! Please! Don't kill me!" she screamed again, but with a little more enthusiasm.

I grabbed my dick at the base and tapped her swollen lips with it. She winced in pain when I hit a tender spot.

I guided myself back within the confines of her mouth, gripped her head, and began to pulverize her trachea.

Ghlup — ghlup — ghlup — ghlup!

Her throat struggled to accommodate my girth and velocity. I grit my teeth and pictured her pussy wrapped around Spider's dick. Rage enflamed me. Her titties swung across her chest as my nuts swung across her chin.

She coughs on the dick, like she's about to puke. I secretly want her to. I propped my left leg onto the bed and dug in deeper. My balls ached. Her eyes wide with warning. Her body jerks, and so does my cock. With a loud grunt, I released my seeds into her belly. And with a retching sound, she released them back onto me.

Ugghhhh!

Before I could step back, yellow-greenish fluids spewed from her mouth and drenched my entire dick. What the fuck? I pulled back, and she threw up again. This time, on the carpet. She kept her head down, unable to look at me due to shame. I see a male's shirt laying on the floor beside the bed.

It must be Spider's, I deduced.

I snatched it up, then wiped my dick clean—just as Demon pokes his head into the room. He looked at Jocelyn and smiled at the sight of her pretty, pink pussy. But then, he noticed the vomit and wrinkled his nose.

"He gave up the location," he said.

Apparently, Spider bought the show Jocelyn had put on. We head into the kitchen. Behind the stove is a false panel. That's where he kept the money and drugs. After we cleaned him out, we left the trio zip-tied and alone to fend for themselves.

Demon and I head straight to his sister Debra's apartment. Debra's a nice little chocolate chick. Slim thick, with a thirty-four-inch ass. She was going to school to be a computer engineer. A good girl. One I felt had a thing for bad boys.

As soon as we entered her crib, I noticed how clean and fresh it smelled. The air was crisp, with a faint scent of lemon. Demon had a key, so we didn't need to knock, but apparently she didn't know that we were there. Either that, or she didn't care, because she came out with a pair of pink cotton shorts so small and tight, I could clearly see the print of her clit ring. The bottom half of her ass cheeks were hanging out. Her pink wife beater hugged her mounds tightly, exposing her hardened nipples. I couldn't help but stare.

She saw us, smiled, then wrinkled her nose. "What is that smell?"

I suddenly felt embarrassed. "My homeboy got drunk and threw up all over me," I half-lied. "I need to hop in the shower, if you don't mind."

She appraised me for a few moments, as if judging my truthfulness. After shrugging her shoulders, she led me to the guest bathroom. I watched as her ass jiggled with each step she took. I could tell she had a big ole, fat-ass pussy. My mouth watered just thinking about how good she would taste sitting on my tongue. I wonder if she knows how to suck dick?

"Bath towels are in the cabinet, washcloths are in the drawer."

"A'ight. Well, thank you . . . Miss Debra."

She smiled. "Whatever, boy. Ain't no telling what you done got into tonight. I know your ass wasn't about to be funking up my spot like that." Her lightheartedness deflected any insult. I chuckled and watched her turn around. Ass wobbling. Coochie chewing up her cotton shorts.

Imma definitely have to find a way to tap that.

I took a nice, hot, long shower, but realized I didn't have any clothes. I wasn't about to throw my soiled linen back on, so I wrapped a towel around my waist and went to search the room Demon uses when he crashes over. Thankfully, no one was in the hallway. I found his room, and after rummaging through his closet, I found something to wear. I didn't have any fresh set of boxers to put on, so I freeballed. (No underwear.) I wasn't 'bout to put on any of Demon's used ones.

When I walked back into the living room, he had everything laid out on the coffee table. Debra was in the kitchen, fixing us a late-night breakfast. After counting out the bread, we realized we hit for seventy bands. After we put up fifteen for Jocelyn, we had twenty thousand more than we expected. Plus, we came up on a brick and a half. Not to mention the guns.

Demon and I split everything down the middle. He kept the mini Draco, and I kept both the pistols. I could hardly concentrate, as Debra pranced around with her coochie on display.

"Here you go, Debra. For allowing us to take care of bidness in your crib," I say, as I hand her a stack.

At first, she looked at it, as if she didn't want to take it. But her better judgment won out.

"Thank you, Rashard." She looked at Demon, expecting him to do the same. At first, he looked like he didn't want to, but then his better judgment won out. After he handed her a stack, Debra retired to her bedroom. I damn near wanted to follow her in there. If Demon wasn't here, I probably would have.

"Here. Give this to bro for me." Demon handed me ten, one-hundred-dollar bills.

"Who?" I asked, genuinely confused.

He frowned his face up, like he couldn't believe I could ask such a thing. "Kay, who else?"

"Oh. Yeah. I'm tripping, dawg. My mind just went somewhere else." I take the money and put it in my pocket. I'm really glad he just gave me the bread, because I really tripped out giving his sister that money.

We dabbed each other up, and I made a move to head outside. As I head to my car, my phone vibrates. It's a text message from Jocelyn.

Jocelyn: Where u at?

Rah: Leaving the homie's crib. 👀

Jocelyn: He doesn't suspect a thing. He thinks it's them niggas from Dead End.

Rah: Bet. U good baby

Jocelyn: Yeah. Till I threw up on yo' dick. Lol

Rah: It's a lot of dick 2 handle

Jocelyn: Boy, whateva. I've been handling that dick since a teenager. Stop playing!

Rah: Fa Shit Sho. I got dat 15 for u. When u want it?

Jocelyn: Give me 10 min. Imma tell him I need to run to the store real quick to get some ointment for my lip. Then we can meet up.

Rah: Facts, just hit me.

Jocelyn: okay love. 🖤

I dropped the phone in the console, and wondered—should I make her give me some of that pussy when she pulls up? Might as well. That way I can send her back home with my dick on her breath and her pussy full of cum.

Chapter 6

Kaydon

I stepped out of my Impala still drunk, having just left the strip club *Bottoms Up.* I hit the alarm and headed to me and Danielle's apartment. A cold chill courses through me, as the wind slaps me across the face. I throw the hood over my head and retreat within myself, hoping to draw some heat from my core.

I pulled out my keys and inserted them. As I step in, the apartment melts the chill from my bones, but there's another chill that settles in my gut. I checked the kitchen. No trace of Danielle. My keys got tossed on the coffee table as I stumbled towards the bedroom.

What sounds like moaning travels into my ears. I quickly blame it on the liquor. But as I approached the bedroom door, the noise increased. My heart thunders in my chest plate. Something was screaming at me, *Don't open the door,* but I couldn't resist the urge. The need.

I pushed it open and my jaw dropped. Danielle's squatting over some nigga, both feet planted on the bed. His dick, pistons in and out of her snatch. Her ass cheeks jiggled and shook with each stroke. I attempted to scream out in anger, but my voice didn't seem to work.

As if sensing my presence, she turned on the dick and caught me standing there. Instead of being startled, stopping, and begging for forgiveness, Danielle only smiles, tilts her head back, and howls that she's cumming.

"OH fuck! He's making me cum! Kay, he's making me cum so hard!"

I feel sick with hatred. I wanted to snatch her ass off ole boy, then beat his ass for disrespecting my home. Then, I would do her the same way. I want to—but both my legs feel as if they weigh three hundred pounds apiece.

So, I'm forced to stay rooted and watch. Watch as my girlfriend leaned forward while reaching back, spreading her ass cheeks apart. I have no choice but to get an unobstructed view of her lover fucking her sopping wet cunt to pieces.

Desperately, I tried to see his face. Something gnawed at the back of my skull. I feel I know his identity, but every time I think I'm about to finally catch a glimpse, Danielle seems to block my view.

Finally, I hear him grunt and groan. I can tell he's about to cum.

"Cum in my pussy, baby. Fill me up with that sweet, tasty nut," she urged him.

He growls and releases billions of sperm cells into my girl's womb. She showered him with kisses as his balls danced and twitched.

Reluctantly, Danielle pulled up, allowing his slimy, cream-coated cock to flop out. Her pussy hole gaped open. She rolled over, and her lover began to sit up. I was finally about to get a chance to see his face and—

Celly . . . Look out, celly!

I opened my eyes. My heart is still rattling in my rib cage. Sweat trickled down the side of my temples. I stare down at my celly from the top bunk.

"Huh?" I asked, groggily.

"You go to chow?"

I'm so disoriented, it takes me a while to realize where I'm at. I glanced at the clock radio on the table. 10:38 a.m. Yea, it's almost chow time.

"Uhh . . . Naw, I'm chilling, bro," I finally told him. He shrugged his shoulders.

"They have chicken patty. Want me bring you back?"

I reached under my mat and handed him my ID. That way, he could scan my card and get my tray. I laid in my bunk as he got himself prepared for chow.

That was the third time I had that same dream about Danielle. Since I've been in prison, she hasn't written or came to see me. Shit, she still hadn't even set the phone up. The Game God must be trying to tell me something. I wish I knew exactly what it was.

As soon as my celly leaves, I jump down and get myself together. After attending to my hygiene, I pour myself a shot of coffee and do a quick little workout to tighten up.

While I'm bird bathing, a sweet-smelling scent enters my nostrils. A woman's fragrance. Sure enough, seconds later, Ms. Dean's standing in front of my cell.

"What you doing back there?"

I know she saw the floor wet and could tell that I'm bathing.

"I'm bird bathing," I replied, slightly agitated.

"Let me see. I need to make sure you don't have any contraband."

"Mann . . . gone on, Ms. Dean. You know a nigga ba—"

"I said, let me see."

She said it a little more forceful that time. I pulled the sheet back, so she could see everything. Her eyes instantly locked onto my dick. I couldn't help it. My shit began to stir and come to life.

Ms. Dean bit her bottom lip slightly and said, "Alright, Snow," before walking off.

Damn, I ain't know she was a freak like that. Since I'd been in prison, I hadn't been messing with any of the guards. Mainly because I didn't want nothing fucking up my appeal.

Claudia found me a lawyer she worked with, who agreed to work on my case. I asked her what he was charging. Her reply was, *"I'll take care of it. Whatever you do, don't tell your brother."*

The way I'm feeling right now, fuck him. Really, fuck everybody else. Well, except for my momma, of course.

Now, Ms. Dean had me thinking 'bout snatching up one of the guards. She was a slim, chocolate chick, with a whole lot of sex appeal. The type, when you look at her, you just *know* she has some good pussy.

I've never been into the jack game. I felt something had to be wrong for you to just pull your dick out and jack on a female guard. But now, I'm thinking that some of these female guards are as sexually frustrated as the inmates. Maybe some of them *do* want to see that dick hiccup and spit. After all, fair exchange ain't never been a robbery.

I finished bathing, then made my way to the dayroom when they ran the next in-and-out. As I'm coming down the stairs, I noticed a cluster of dudes clamoring around the fence. Each of them trying to get at Ms. Dean.

I shake my head as I walk by. "Excuse me," I say, while discreetly making eye contact with her. But I won't stop. As I walked off, I felt her eyes boring into the back of my head. If she wants a G to pull up, she gone have to get rid of them suckas.

I act as if I'm getting on one of the blue phones attached to the wall in the dayroom, just so I could have an excuse to look her way. Sure enough, I caught her eyeing me down. The crazy thing is, she wasn't trying to hide.

My eyes danced over her fan club to let her know what's blocking my path. She took the hint and told them all to sit down. I left the coast clear for ten minutes before I decided to approach.

When I finally did, I could see her demeanor. She was already mine.

"Wassup, Ms. Dean? Why you keep staring at me?"

I don't waste no time or pull no punches. I know she wasn't expecting me to call her out on that.

"What you mean? It's my job to look at you."

I scoff at that. "Oh yeah? Well, let that be the reason. Don't get me wrong, I don't mind. But if you gone stare, don't be scared to speak."

"Who said I'm scared to speak? I'm talking right now, ain't I?"

"Yeah, but you're not talking my language."

She looked sort of perplexed at my declaration. "And what's your language?"

With assuredness, I state, "Money!"

Her head jerks slightly at my bold and utter confidence. Most dudes would have danced around the subject until they felt the water was warm. That may work for some, but for me, I feel sometimes you have to trust your instincts. And mine told me—she'd been in the bag.

Ms. Dean and I talked for about thirty minutes straight. Everything from her family to her reason for working at the prison. Eventually, we discussed her finances. I told her how I got railroaded and I wanted to put some bread together to get a lawyer. I know Claudia said she would take care of it, but I wasn't about to depend on no one to broker my freedom but me.

I noticed dudes started lightweight hating. Whining about an in-and-out, when it hadn't even been an hour. I asked her if she had an Instagram she could give me. She said she had to make one, but she would do it that night and bring it to me the next time she worked the block.

I don't have a phone, but I knew one of my celly's homeboys did. He'd asked me before if I wanted to rent some hours on it. When shift change came, I was super excited about the prospect. I didn't mess with too many niggas. Really, when it came to talking 'bout shit like that, I rode with my celly. After I laced him up on the encounter with Ms. Dean, he wrote a kite to his homeboy and told him we would start needing the phone every night to run a play. The homeboy agreed.

"Whateva you need, I got everything," he kept reiterating. So, that was the plan. My celly supplied the work, and I worked Ms. Dean.

Later that night, I checked the tablet. I had four new snap and sends. All of them were from Claudia. This time, she had on an all-red, form-fitting dress. That bad boy was hugging all of her curves. If I had to guess, she looked like she was going out.

I noticed I also had a regular e-message letter. I opened it up. She said she was heading out for her homegirl's birthday and wanted to send me a couple of pics of her dressed up. I opened up the other two snap and sends. Two of them were of her in the dress, but one was of her in a towel, doing her makeup.

Honestly, I had no idea what to make of it. She was my brother's wife. My sister-in-law. At the same time, she was the only one besides my T-Lady pulling up, checking on a real nigga. What was I supposed to do, turn her away? Run her off, out of some misplaced loyalty to my brother, who doesn't write, send money, or bother to come visit? Fuck that!

I write her back and tell her thanks for the pics and I hope they had a good time. I also tell her I need to talk to her and when would be a good time to call? She'd set the phone up, as well as put money on the account for me, but I told her I would only call if and when she told me to. I didn't need my brother to find out. I know he'd be on some hating-ass shit.

Once I was done writing, I put the tablet up and laid it down. For the first time since I'd been locked up, I felt alive. The crazy thing is, I think it had to do with the fact I was able to hustle again. The opportunity to do what I was born to do and be who I truly was. A hustling-ass nigga.

The next day, Ms. Dean did in fact work our pod. She did as she said she would and brought me her IG account. "From now on, we won't do too much talking while you're at work. Imma let them other niggas get the air time. Imma get mine, while you at the house relaxing." I can tell she was a bit disappointed about me telling her that, but she'd already started respecting my lead.

I spent the rest of the day in my cell, waiting for her to head home. My celly grabbed the phone from his homeboy, and I hit her in her DM. We spent the next three hours enjoying each other's conversation. By the time we stopped messaging, she was committed to the grind. All I had to do now was put it in her hands.

Danielle

"Girl. Say what? Who's supposed to be performing tonight?"

"Bitch. The pride and joy of the East. Who else? Lo-Life!" Andrea sounded like she was about to blow a fuse, she was so excited.

"But I thought he was on tour?" I asked.

"He is. He's sliding through the city twice. He'll be back in two months, but a bitch can't wait that long," Andrea's thirsty ass whined.

"Pssht. Damn," I realized. "I gotta work. They got a bitch working overtime," I add, disappointedly.

"Work? D, what are you talking 'bout right now? You can work any day of the week. Work? Yeah, Imma work alright. Work my ass backstage. Then, Imma try and work this ass, pussy, and mouth on that nigga's dick. You talking 'bout a nine-to-five? Bitch, this is a once-in-a-lifetime."

She made all the perfect sense in the world, and to be honest with myself, I really did want to go to that concert. That nigga Lo-Life is my favorite rapper of all time. Then, he's from where I'm from, so that just puts the icing on the cake. We all watched him come up in the streets. When it came to authentic, street music, he was that nigga.

"D, why don't you pull up on that old manager of yours and tell him you're sick or something?"

"'Cause I told him that last time you drugged a bitch somewhere," I answered back.

"Well, I don't know what to tell you. I got two tickets and if you're not gonna go, Imma hit up Raquel and see what she's talking 'bout."

"Raquel? Raquel? Come on, Drea, you know she don't fuck with rap like that."

"Okay, but shit. What you want me to do, throw them in the trash?"

"Look, give me . . ." I looked at the time. 1:37 p.m. . . . "Give me till three-thirty. I'm supposed to get off at five. If I can't make something shake by then, go ahead and take Raquel," I tell her.

"A'ight D. You got till three-thirty."

"Bet, bitch. Let me get on top of that. Bye." When Kay went to jail, I had to get a job. Seeing as I didn't have a record, it didn't take long. One of my uncles put me on with an old associate of his, named Carl. He had a mechanic shop, as well as the BBQ spot everybody went to. Since I was a "friend of the family," he gave me a lil' more flexibility than other employees. Still, I couldn't get away with murder.

Working at Carl's BBQ was cool. My job title was waitress/hostess. The tips were great. Everybody pulled up at Carl's. As soon as someone pulls up that recognizes me, they immediately ask about Kaydon. Many of them even give me money to send to him. I guess they felt bad about what transpired with him.

Speaking of Kay, I haven't talked to him in over a year. Not since he left the County. I still care about him, but forty years is just too long. The way I figure it, we might as well go our separate ways now. Why waste five to ten years riding the time out with him when I know I'mma leave him anyway?

I guess people just expected for me to be holding him down, because they're always trying to approach me about his well-being. Sometimes, I'm tempted to tell them, "Your guess is as good as mine." Instead, I go with the flow, take the money, and tell them, "I'll let him know you asked about him." Am I wrong for that?

Anyway, I needed to figure out how I was gonna get out of working overtime. Even though Carl's my Uncle Tony's homeboy, he doesn't like to cut me any slack. He said if he showed favoritism, his other employees wouldn't respect him anymore. The only way I could think of was getting someone to cover my shift.

There were only two other waitresses on the roster, and to be honest, neither one of them liked me. I waited until the traffic died down before I headed out back to Carl's office. Knock, knock, knock.

"Come in." His deep baritone voice boomed through the door. I timidly twist, then push it open. I stepped in. Luther V could be heard crooning over the stereo system.

Carl, or Big Carl, as some people called him, was perched behind his Oakwood desk, going over some paperwork. To be in his mid-fifties, he was still a strikingly handsome man. Salt-and-peppered hair, with the matching goatee. His light brown eyes sparkled with mischief, even though he had a deadly and serious demeanor. From what I heard from her Uncle, Carl had come up the hard way. Blood, sweat, tears, and more blood. Now, he was legit.

He looked up from his desk. Reading glasses teetered on the bridge of his nose. "Hey Danielle, how can I help you?"

"Hey, Mr. Smith, can I—"

"Carl . . . Call me Carl, Danielle. Our people go back too far, for us to be that formal with each other, even in a work setting."

"Okay. My bad then, Carl. Umm, I know I'm supposed to be working overtime tonight, but something came up, and I really, really need off. I understand I can't take off unless someone is willing to take my shift, but . . . ." That's about as far as I got when I rehearsed my speech. I really didn't know what the solution would be, I just knew that I needed to try. I needed to go see my nigga perform.

Carl just sat there staring at me for a long while. So long, in fact, I started to feel self-conscious. Suddenly, he spoke up. "You know, me and your momma used to have a thing back in the day." I was shocked to hear that, and I know he could tell.

"Yeah? My uncle never told me that."

"He probably wouldn't. He didn't approve of us. I was knee-deep and dangerously in the streets back then. He just didn't want her getting caught up in no bullshit." I nodded, as if I understood completely.

All of a sudden, I noticed how Carl looked at me in my tight-fitting uniform pants. His eyes kept lingering on my obvious camel toe. I wonder. "So, why did you and my mom stop messing around?" I asked, with a lil' more sultriness in my voice.

"Well, to be honest, your daddy. He was the only man, besides your uncle, I respected. When he laid claim to your momma, I backed up."

"Do you miss her?" I asked.

Carl chuckled. His voice softened, almost to a whisper. "Every day I see you, it brings back fond memories."

I decided to push a lil' bit further. "Oh yeah? What type of memories?" Something was telling me, ole Carl wanted a trip down memory lane.

"Well, I don't know if I should talk about these kinds of things with her . . . daughter."

"Come on now, Carl, we're both grown. Shit, I'm probably older now than my momma was, back when y'all were . . . fucking." Hearing me voice it out loud did something to him. I peeped him reaching under the desk to readjust himself.

I slowly walked around, making sure I held eye contact with him the entire time. "I bet I know what you've missed, Carl," I purred, less than a foot away from him.

His eyes are now locked onto my gap. He subconsciously wets his lips. His breathing became haggard. He swallowed heavily, as I reached for the sides of his head. I caressed his ear, tracing the lobe with the tip of my finger. "You've missed the taste of her kitty cat, don't you?" I whispered.

He didn't say yes, but he swallowed again. I pulled his head slowly into my crotch. The tip of his nose touched the zipper on my uniform pants. "Take a whiff, Carl, see if you can smell how delicious my kitty is." Carl intakes a great big breath. He shuddered and moaned at the same time.

I reached down, unbuckled, then unzipped my pants. I worked them off my hips, until I'm able to step out of them. There I stand, white socks, black thong panties, and a red and black Carl's BBQ T-shirt on. "You wanna see if this pussy tastes as good as my momma's did?" He gave me the slightest of nods. "I need you to say it, Carl. Tell me you wanna see if my pussy tastes as good as my momma's."

He looked up with pleading eyes. Once he saw I wouldn't give him what he craved until he said it, he submitted. "I wanna see if your pussy tastes as good as your momma's did."

I swept the paperwork off his desk. They go flying in all different directions. "Scoot back," I told him. He rolled his office chair back, giving me the room I needed. I stepped in front of him, then hopped onto the desk. Each of my feet is placed squarely on the arms of the chair. I leaned back on my elbows, looked him in the eyes, and said, "Come find out."

Carl wasted no time. He pulled the crotch of my panties to the side, licked my slit, from the mouth of my pussy to the tip of my clit. Now, it was my turn to moan. His large and calloused hands gripped the backs of my thighs, pushing my legs back. My coochie popped out, and he began to feast.

His long tongue snaked its way through my folds. Juices splashed against his chin. Wet smacking sounds, and Luther, are all that's being heard. I looked down between my legs and saw the top of his head. Salt and pepper, with a slight bald spot in the center. Just the thought of those same lips sucking on my momma's coochie before had me ready to blow.

Carl pulled the hood on my clit back. His full lips blanketed my button, while his tongue danced around the tip.

I shivered. My nut began to bubble up. Carl grunted into my pussy, gripping my thighs tightly as I rode his face. "Ooh shit. Ooh shit. Ooooh Carl, I'm finna cum, daddy. Fuuccckk, I'm finna cuummmm!" He sucked and pulled harder on my clit. The bubble popped, and I flooded his mouth with sweet cum.

Euphoric bliss took over my being. Carl continued to lap at my coochie, pulling on each one of my sex lips until my orgasm subsided. I'm breathless. If momma got this type of head, I know she was distraught when she had to leave him alone. Carl finally detached himself from my box. Mouth greasy and glistening with my copious cum, he smiled up at me.

"Well?" I ask him. "What's the verdict? Is it just as good?"

He licked the corners of his mouth, trying to sop up the rest of the honeydew. After smacking his lips, he said, "Better!"

My face lit up with a smile. "Whatever, Carl, you're just saying that." He kissed my coochie three more times before he sat all the way up.

"Naw, I'm serious. I will definitely want another round of that."

"Well, that could be arranged if I really need to take tonight off," I proposed.

"Well, I think that could be arranged," he mimicked. That's how I was able to get the rest of the night off.

Now, I'm standing in front of a full-length mirror, clad in a black-laced thong and bra set. Thirty minutes before Andrea is supposed to pull up, I still don't know what I wanna wear. I consider wearing some form-fitting jeans, but something is telling me, I need to be accessible. Fuck it!

Since red's Lo-Life's color, I elected to rock a red, silk Fendi dress. The hem is so short, my ass cheeks peek out the bottom of it. With some white Louboutin, a white Fendi clutch, I sprayed on some *Nude by Rihanna* and I'm ready to go.

My doorbell rang. Just in time. I swung the door open. Andrea stood there, in an all-black, low-cut, mid-thigh Chanel dress. It's silk also, so it's pretty much see-through. I could easily see, she doesn't have a bra on. Her nipples are already poking. Her areolas, dark and resembled half a dollar. I snatched off my bra and we headed out the door.

"You trynna smoke something before we go in?" she asked, as we approached the venue. I shrugged my shoulders.

"Pull the ashtray out, there's a half blunt in there." As I pulled out the ashtray, she dug in the center console and retrieved a lighter. "Here, gone, spark up."

I'm not a big smoker, but when I do, I don't like to smoke no bullshit. "What is this?" I asked suspiciously, examining the half-smoked blunt.

"OG Kush," she replied proudly. I put the flame to the tip and took the first two pulls to the head. Ten minutes later, I'm lit as Times Square. My whole body's tingling.

We pulled up to the venue, and that bitch was packed. The show didn't start until 9:00 p.m. I looked at the clock. It was barely 8:30. We found a place to park and made the walk towards the front. On the way there, we eyed three deliciously looking hood niggas. One, tall and dark, with a bald head. Another was brown-skinned, taper fade, with spinning waves. The last one had a red complexion, bald fade, with a goatee. Each of them were covered in tattoos.

To be completely honest, the way I was feeling, any one of them could get it. The way Andrea was looking, I think she felt the same way. After some serious eye-fucking, they approached. The tall dark one was the first to speak. He must be the Alpha, I told myself.

"We don't mean to hold you ladies up, but if it's not too much trouble, we'd like y'all's number, so we could maybe link up after the show."

I looked at Andrea and smiled before I returned my attention back to him. "You're not gonna tell us your name? We're supposed to give our numbers to complete strangers?"

"Oh, my bad. You're absolutely right. Where are my manners? My name is Jack." He pointed to the brown-skinned one next. "This is my cousin X.O. and this other gentleman is named Face."

The other two men outstretched their hands in a formal greeting.

Drea and I shook their hands and introduced ourselves. "I'm Danielle, and this is my sister Andrea. And yes, y'all can have my number." I exchanged contact information with the trio and agreed to catch up with them later. Since Drea was in a relationship, we agreed she would go through me to deal with them. I'm pretty sure if they impressed her enough, she'd find a way to link up with them herself.

Once we separated from the guys, she turned to me and asked, "So, which one do you want?"

I bit my bottom lip. "Girl, I don't know. All three of them look scrumptious."

"I know, right. I was thinking the same thing."

"We gone just let them choose then," I told her, as we found our section. It wasn't lost on me that it was three of them and only two of us. I didn't know how Andrea felt, but I was with all the action.

***

The concert was off the chain. The crowd went ape shit when my nigga Lo hit the stage. We didn't even know it, but the East was deep up in that bitch. From Baytown to Denver

Harbor. He definitely put on for the hood. When he performed his street anthem, *Legend In My Hood*, I damn near passed out. I would have done anything for a backstage pass. Alas, once the concert was over, we made our way through the thick crowd and back out to the parking lot.

My phone began to vibrate in my purse. I pulled it out and saw it was a text message: *Can we call?* I showed the phone to Drea. "Wassup, you trynna let them niggas slide, or what?"

She shrugged. "Bitch, I'm with whatever," she bragged.

"Bet that," I responded, before I texted back: *Call now.* A second later, my phone rang. Jack was on the line. After a brief conversation, we agreed to meet up at Waffle House.

As we ate, I noticed Jack and his cousin XO can't stop staring at a bitch. My kitty began to purr, as I thought about getting double penetrated. That's one thing I wish Kay would have been open to. When it came to bringing another woman into our bed, I was down for it. Soon as I asked him to bless my game by bringing another set of dick and balls, the nigga would look at me as if I'm off my rocker.

"So, what's the plan?" I asked the trio.

"Well, that's up to y'all. If y'all want the night to end, we can go our separate ways. If you and your girl trynna get active, we can slide to the room and do it big," Face challenged.

I looked to Drea, as if we hadn't already decided what we were going to do hours ago. Then, a thought occurred. "Well, we can do that if . . . Y'all are willing to compensate a bitch for her time and energy." Drea looked at me in surprise. She didn't see that coming, but according to the sly smile on her face, I saw she approved.

The trio looked at each other. A silent agreement was made. "How much?" I looked to Drea. She gave me a look, as if to say, *Don't look at me, bitch. This was your bright idea.*

I did a quick assessment of their known assets: the car, the clothes, the jewels. I shot my shot. "A band apiece for me an' my girl. If y'all want to see some girl-on-girl, then that's fifteen hundred a piece."

Andrea's mouth dropped. I honestly don't know where that came from, so I know she was shocked as hell to hear it. Her and I had never even gotten close to kissing, much less fucking around with each other. To her credit, she doesn't say anything and just goes with the flow. She trusted me to walk her through this uncharted territory.

For a second, I think I've scared them off. Until they all three nod and pull out a stack apiece. Each one of them laid a thousand dollars on the table. Three thousand total.

There it was. It was settled. By the end of the night, I would have the scent of dick and pussy on my breath. After Drea and I scooped up the money, the guys paid for our meals, and we headed to the hotel. Everyone eager to see what the rest of the night would bring.

Chapter 7

Andrea

"Girl. You. Are. A. Motherfucker." I can't believe this bitch Danielle just sold my coochie. What's crazy is, I'm not offended by it. In fact, I'm excited, intrigued, and horny as hell.

"Bitch, I figured if we gone buss our shit open, we might as well make them niggas buss open their wallets. Ain't no stupid shit going on," she reasoned.

"I know that's right." Then, I thought about it. "But wait, them niggas paid us three bands. They're trynna see some girl-on-girl."

Danielle gave me a side glance. "We ain't gotta do it. If you want, we can shoot them the other band back. I was just—"

"No, no, no, I'm gucci. This ain't the first time I'm gonna dine on some cat. I'm just saying, I didn't know your flavor," I assured her. I done had my fair share of pussy. Much more than the average bitch, I'm sure.

"Girl, I'm good. Fuck around and have your ass climbing up the walls," she bragged.

"Oh yeah. We'll see." I accepted her challenge.

She paused and realized something. "How many rubbers you got?"

"I got three, but let's stop at the store real quick. We need to get us a box," I suggested. She agreed and began to text, asking them to pull over at the nearest gas station. After snatching a couple of boxes, we headed to the Choice Inn.

Even though they reserved the room for the whole night, Danielle and I wasted no time getting down to business. They sat back and watched us play with each other first. I took the time to smell her coochie. Surprised, she was still somewhat fresh, considering we were at a packed concert hours before.

I took the tip of my tongue and penetrated her hole, caressing the insides of her walls with it. Her sweet and tangy essence laid heavy on my taste buds. She moaned as I worked my way up her slit, stopping at her swollen nub. I peeled her hood back, and her pearl popped out, like a king-size Tic Tac. I covered it completely with my mouth and began to assault her button with the heavy swipes from my tongue.

Her whole body began to vibrate. I pushed two fingers into her snatch and massaged her g-spot. Danielle bucked within my grasp. "Oh my Gawd, Oh my Gawd, Sssshit! It feels soooo good," she confessed. I trapped her clit between my lips and applied more suction. Her pussy walls clamped down around my fingers. Her body began convulsing. "Oh shit, I'm cumming, I'm cumming, I'm cummmingg!"

Danielle's juices skeeted into my mouth. I drank every drop, greedily smacking on her sex lips in the process. My mouth was a mess. I moaned and hummed over her clit, causing her to shake and jerk from the sensitivity.

Finally, she pushed my head away, begging for a reprieve. I disengaged, crawled up her body, until my own fat, juicy cunt was hovering over her mouth.

As I held onto the headboard, I looked down at her, trapped between my legs, and I fed her what she asked for. I wound and twerked, twisted and jerked, until it became too much. I exploded onto her face. "Aww fuck, Ssshit!" I flushed out my pussy right into her waiting mouth.

Before I had time to recover, XO stood on the bed, in nothing but a pair of Nike socks. I felt Danielle moan into my coochie. I turned around and caught sight of Jack, sliding his condom-coated cock into her wet, tight cunt.

I don't know where Face is, but I returned my attention back to the dick in front of me. XO grabbed himself at the base with his left hand, wagging his semi-erect dick in my face. With his right, he grabbed the back of my head, pulling me forward. I opened up wide to receive him. "Mmmmm," I moaned with delight. His cock fit perfectly within the confines of my mouth. *Ghlup—Ghlup—Ghlup—Ghlup.* He fucked my throat at a steady pace.

Suddenly, I'm pulled off of Danielle and positioned at the edge of the bed. "Turn around," XO ordered. I did what he asked. Face appeared out of nowhere, sat in front of me, and I took him into my mouth. I heard a condom wrapper being ripped open. Moments later, I felt his long and heavy dick open me up. I gasped and groaned as he began to buss my coochie open.

For the next four hours, the three of them fucked Danielle and I every which way but loose. I ate so much cum, I might be able to shit out a baby. I'll say this though, that bitch Danielle can take some dick. We each got double penetrated at one point or another. I sucked Jack's dick, fresh out of her asshole. She did the same with Face, after he got done punching in my backdoor.

When it was said and done, I was completely exhausted. I dropped Danielle off at her crib and headed to my momma's house. There was no way I was going home in the state I was in. AD would surely put his foot in my ass. I'll just tell him I came to spend the night with our son, AJ.

As I pulled up to my momma's crib, I saw a green pickup truck in the driveway. She must have company, I thought, as I parked, hopped out, and headed to the front door. It was almost five in the morning, so chances of her being up were slim to none.

I unlocked the door and immediately headed to the shower. I spent twenty minutes washing my ass before grabbing a bath towel and wrapping it around myself. I opened the door and headed toward my old bedroom.

Imagine my surprise when I hit the corner and ran smack into a butt-naked, dark-skinned, dread-wearing, big-dick-swinging man. "Oh my...Shit!" He blurted out, trying to find something to cover up all that cock. "I ain't know anybody was here," he tried to explain.

"It's okay, I'm her daughter. She didn't know I was coming," I absolved him. Sensing my lack of embarrassment, he seemed to summon up some courage. Standing at his full six-foot, four-inch height, I got my first good look at him. The nigga had to be in his late twenties, early thirties at the most. My momma is about to be sixty next year.

I don't blame her though. Based on what he's packing, I know he'd been knocking the dust, cobwebs, and whatever else she had backed up, out of her pussy. I realized he was staring intensely at my chest. I looked down. My nipples were hard as steel bars. He could see them poking through the thick, cotton towel. My eyes instinctively traveled down to his dick. It twitched, and I jumped. Oh, no, no, no, no. I gotta get out of here. "Excuse me," I say, as I hurriedly head into my old room. I'm glad my son has his own room in the house.

As soon as the door's closed and locked, I laid back on the bed. Still damp from the shower, I played in my pussy until I buss a fat ass nut all over my fingers. Wishing I could trade places with my momma, only for one night.

AD

"Say, Dame, it better be some money there tonight. I'm not trynna come all the way to the South, just to win a band or two," I tell him, as I merged onto the freeway. It's a little after nine o'clock. Most niggas might be headed to the club, or even to some lil' bitch's spot. Me, I'm trynna come up off some skill and a lil' bit of luck.

I've been shooting dice since I was eleven years old. Middle school. We used to skip class and shoot dice in the restroom. Back then, it was ones and fives. Sometimes, you might see a ten or twenty. Now, a nigga shooting hundreds, sometimes thousand-dollar shots.

I've been all over the city gambling. Every shack you could think of, I've done been in that muthafucka. Sometimes I lose, but most of the time, I win.

See, dice does pertain a level of luck. Where the skill comes in, you have to know when to ride with the dice, and when to buck them. If your shot is off, don't force it. Wait until you catch fire, then bet big. I was headed to Ray's gambling shack for the night. It's usually good for at least fifteen bands. Still, I gotta give Dame a hard time about it.

"AD, you know it's gonna be worth it, my nigga. Ray's always got at least ten to fifteen, every time them thangs come out."

"Who says?" I teased him.

"You and I both know that's facts," he countered.

Dame is one of my longtime gambling buddies. I'm not gonna say we're best of friends, because I'm trynna take his money too, but if one of us wins, we'll kick back some bread to the other. That way, they could scratch back. Maybe a band or two. "Yeah, yeah. We'll see. I'm almost there. Give me like fifteen more minutes," I said, before hanging up the phone.

Before I turn my screen off, I saw I had a text message from one of my jump-offs, named Kiera. Realizing she's from the South, I went ahead and called her. "Hello?"

"Wassup?"

"Hey, baby," she sang out. "What you doing?"

"I'm 'bout to walk into Ray's."

"Boy, what you know 'bout Ray's? That's down the street from my house."

"Yeah, I know. I'm 'bout to shoot some dice."

She smacked her lips. "Pssht. Why you ain't tell me you was over here?"

"To be honest, my nigga Dame just told me they was shooting tonight," I lied. I been knew it was a game, for two days now.

"Okay. Well, what you gone do afterwards?"

"I don't know. Why, wassup?" I asked, baiting her in.

"Boy, don't play with me. You know wassup. You haven't pulled up on a bitch in almost a month," she complained.

"I'm not tripping on sliding through, but you know how long these dice games be. A nigga might not leave this bitch till four or five in the morning."

"I don't care what time it is. If I'm sleep, wake me up. I'm not letting you leave this side of town until you swing by and drop off some of that dick."

I had to smile. Whoever said women don't think about sex as much as men, is full of shit. "I got you. Just make sure you keep your phone by you."

"I will. Oh, and don't lose all your money. When you lose, you fuck a bitch like you just wanna buss and burn. When you win, you stay up in that pussy like it's a penthouse apartment."

"Hopefully, I'll be moving on up, like the Jeffersons then," I joked, before disconnecting the call.

When I pulled up to the parking lot, it reminded me of an after-hour spot. I saw a mixture of vehicles: pickup trucks, old-school slabs, and a few six-figure foreigns.

Ray's had been up and running for over twenty-five years. Never been shut down, or shot up. For a black-owned business, that meant something.

I waltzed through the front door after paying the doorman, Big Russell. Ray's was one of the only shacks I know that could get away with charging you fifty to a hundred dollars to get in. Trust, though, it was well worth it.

They had two separate tables set up. One table was straight out the cup. The other, freestyle, but you had to switch the dice every ten shots, or when someone fell off. I watched the scene for about ten minutes, until Dame found me. "Wassup nigga? What it's looking like?" I asked, trynna gauge which table I should sit down at.

He pointed to the cup table. "That nigga Jim Bo's been cleaning up. He's been hot for the last twenty minutes. Tens and foes, is what's been getting him paid."

I nodded. "What about the other table?" I asked.

"Ain't nobody really took charge. A couple niggas went on some runs, but nothing over five or six points." I made my decision. Even though Jim Bo's due to fall off soon, he's too savvy of a hustler not to know that. So, he wouldn't put it all on the line. He'd make a nigga claw tooth and nail until he got back hot again. The way you get him is to wait until you're hot, then poke at his pride. He'll feel as though he could force you to fall off by bulldogging your bets. I need to pick up steam first.

I headed to the bar and swapped out cash for chips. That's another reason niggas like Ray's. We don't gamble cash. Everything's transferred to chips now. They used to do cash, but a while back, some nigga came in and brought ten bands worth of counterfeit with him. Ever since then, Ray made you buy chips. While you gambled, he inspected your bread. That way, whoever won could be assured everything was on the up and up. As I pulled up to the hostess station, I spotted this lil' brown thing named Rhonda. "Hey, AD," she flirted. I had popped her once, but she ended up feeling bad about it because she had a boyfriend at the time. Now, she looked like she wanted another dose.

"Wassup wit it? Let me get six?"

"How you want it?"

"Uhh. You know what, just mix it up," I told her. Rhonda gave me six bands in chips. Everything from five-dollar chips to five-hundred-dollar chips.

Before I left, she blurted out, "I'm single now."

I turned back around. "Oh yeah. Well, call me tomorrow and we can link up." She nodded, obviously pleased with herself for taking the initiative. To be honest, I'mma buss her up a couple of times, then send her on her way. She already let me fuck while she had a whole nigga at the house. I know for sure, she can't be trusted.

As soon as I pulled up at the freestyle table, I went to work. Things started off slow, but once I found my stroke, I noticed I was up like seven or eight bands. I could have left then, but I had a personal vendetta against Jim Bo.

A couple of months ago, the old nigga took me for close to ten bands. Then, to add insult to injury, he snatched up this pretty lil' female from Waco, named Iesha, from me. Naw, naw. Not tonight! I wasn't about to leave until I cleared the table and cleaned house.

After three hours, there was nobody left but me and Jim Bo. He decided to come join me at the freestyle table. Probably because I was doing a whole lot of flexing. Every time I hit a point, I would scream out, "I'm the greatest!" Or, I might hit them with that NBA Jam, "Boomshakalaka! He's on fiiirrrrreeeee!"

There's nothing that could get under an old-school nigga's skin quicker than a young nigga who's smelling his piss. But yeah, it didn't take long for me and old Jim Bo to lock horns. For the first twenty minutes, he chewed through my stash. I knew I had to be down, at least five bands. But then, I came roaring back.

I also noticed I kept hitting fives and nines on the dice. So, I got bold. I started giving him bets that I only five. All craps. He felt like that was a sucker bet. I popped him for a band like that, three times in a row. Then, it was hard to stop.

By the time 3:45 a.m. came, I'd broken Jim Bo for everything he had. Not counting the six bands I came with, I was up sixteen thousand, four hundred and thirty dollars. I had an otherworldly aura about myself. My body wouldn't stop trembling. It felt like I was on an X-pill.

I hit up Kiera to give her the good news. I tried to find Dame, but he disappeared somewhere. I guess he doesn't want his Juug, I told myself. As I made my way to the parking lot, I don't know if I was tripping or not, but something seemed off. My spider senses were going haywire. I looked around the parking lot. It's practically empty. I jumped in my whip, cranked the engine up, but sat there for a second. Trying my best to shake the jitters off.

I reached under my seat and grabbed my HK 9mm pistol. I made sure one was in the chamber before I sat it back down on my lap. Just as I turned out the lot, my phone began to chime. Kiera's calling. I debated whether or not to head over to her spot. Something felt off, but I didn't know what it was. Against my better judgment, I pushed towards her crib.

When I pulled up to her spot, she was outside waiting on me. She was rocking a pink salmon-colored robe, with some pink furry slippers. Her braids were tied into a ponytail. Kiera isn't the baddest bitch I done messed with, but she's the type of chick that makes it easy for you to be around. She rarely sweats a nigga 'bout the small stuff. She cooks, and when a nigga spends the night, she washes a nigga's socks, boxers, wife beaters, and tees. Add to that, she loved sucking dick and her pussy stayed wet.

My first mind's to leave my money in the car, but I second-guessed myself and brought it with me. I divided it up and stuffed all four pockets full. Instead, I left my pistol under the front seat.

I hopped out and approached her. "Hey, baby," she cooed, as she gave me a hug. I reached up under her robe and palmed her ass cheeks, sliding my finger between her crack and up under her snatch. No panties. I continued to rub my finger through her slit from the back.

"Okay, boy, don't start if you not ready to finish," she warned.

I whispered in her ear, "I know you feel that muthafucka poking you in the stomach."

"Mmmm," is all she said, as she took my hand and led me into the house. Her crib has always been clean and immaculate. That's another thing I loved about her.

"You hungry?"

"What, you gone fix me something to eat?"

"You know I will," she responded.

"Sure." Kiera headed off into the kitchen, as I stripped down to my wife beater and black and red Polo boxer briefs.

Moments later, she returned with a breakfast burrito wrap—eggs, sausage, bacon, with peppers and onions. As I bit into my burrito, Kiera stripped off her robe and dropped to her knees in front of me. I looked down at her inquisitively.

"While you eat, I'm gone eat."

She reached into my waistband and pulled my dick out. I couldn't do anything else but shake my head and continue to eat. Kiera gripped my dick and stuffed her mouth full of my Jimmy Dean. Did I already say she loved to suck dick? If I did, that was an understatement.

Her spit dripped and dribbled down the sides of my shaft. *Ghlup — Ghlup — Ghlup — Ghluuupppp.* She pushed my rod to the back of her throat and held me there. Her tonsils danced across the helmet of my cock.

"Fuuuccckk. Sssshit," I hissed. Putting my nearly done burrito wrap back down on the plate, I tilted my head back, grabbed hers, and surrendered to the bliss. The way Kiera sucked dick was like a masterpiece. Timeless! I felt my balls begin to ache, and I knew I was 'bout to blow.

BOOM!

The front door caved in—knocked off its hinges.

I saw it, but before I could react, I'm getting smacked with the barrel of a pistol.

Thwack!

My whole world spun, flipped upside down.

Kiera, just now seeing what was going on, decided to try and scream. But a vicious blow to the head with the handle of the pistol left her knocked out.

My vision blurred. My head wouldn't stop ringing. One of the two masked men had his gun pointed at me.

"Where's the money at, nigga?"

The side of my face was bleeding. The wound throbbed as blood pumped out of it. I just stared at them, disgusted that I left my strap in the car.

"Oh, so you wanna play tough?" He reached back to bring the handle of the pistol across my forehead, but I flinched and was able to bring my hand up—enough so that I deflected some of the blow.

It still somewhat connected, splitting my forehead open.

"Aggghh fuucckk!" I growled out in agony.

The second gunman finally had enough smarts to check my pants pocket.

"Got it!" he blurted out with excitement.

"Bet. Let's get the fuck outta here."

As I laid on the couch bleeding, my drawers down, my dick still out, I watched them run out with over twenty bands of mine.

That's not even the worst part.

I know who did it.

Chapter 8

Demon

It had been a week since the homie AD got robbed over at ole girl Kiera's spot. First thing out my mouth was, "We shoulda stretched that bitch out." But AD swear up and down she ain't had shit to do with it. A'ight then. If he said it, I'ma fall back.

Rah, him and me, are parked across the street from some apartments called Royal Palms. The apartments are small as fuck. Plus, them hoes are raggedy as hell. *Straight slums.* My type of setting.

I'm in the backseat of the Ford Explorer we rented—for a fifty slab and a zip of K-2. The mini Draco we scored off that play with Spider is sitting on my lap. I slapped a fresh fifty-round clip in that bitch, ready to get to the bidness. AD and Rah are in the front seat, going over logistics. *Who's in the house? Where's the exit? Where's the nearest freeway?* I'll let them handle all that. When it's time for me to do what I do best, it'll get done. Every time.

Apparently, Rah fucked with some female over there. Her job was to buy some wet from them niggas, let us know how many of them were in the spot, and where in the spot they were located. I checked my G-Shock. She was five minutes late.

Suddenly, Rah's phone rang.

"That's her," he announced. "Finally."

"Hello? . . . Yea, okay . . . Just make sure you follow the script. A'ight."

Rah hung up, and we were eagerly awaiting the verdict. He turned to us.

"She said it's three niggas in there. One of them is on the couch with a chopstick on his lap. One nigga's in the back room, and the other is in the kitchen, fucking with the work, bottling up the dip."

"So, what's the play?" I asked. "Who do I need to spank?"

"We gone kick in the door. Demon, you hit the nigga on the couch. I'ma tag the one in the kitchen, and AD, you go straight for your boy. You gone have to be quick. Soon as the nigga hear them thangs go off, he gone be on point."

We had our assignments. I triple-checked my shit and flipped the beam on and off. Everything was in working order.

We hopped out and made our way to the apartments. It's one-thirty in the morning. Everyone's still out and about clubbing. The projects are unusually quiet for this time of night. We make it to the gate and around the corner. As we got closer to the dude's door, Rah looked up. One of the upstairs apartments had their blinds opened and their lights on. That was the sign—the street leading to the apartments was clear and free of police.

Rah positioned himself at the left of the door, me at the right, and AD in the center. AD was doing the honors. With a drop step, his right foot connected with the center of the door, close to the door handle.

BOOM!

I was the first to go in. The couch is to the right, so I sweep the stick around. When my green infrared beam lands on its target, I finger-fucked the trigger.

Pap. Pap. . .

The 7.62s spin, land, and dismount like an Olympic gymnast.

Dude on the couch didn't even have a chance to grab his strap before his head exploded. A grayish-red mist hit the back wall like graffiti.

Bocka—bocka!

I turned and saw a flash of light emit from the kitchen. My heart skips a beat. I upped my chopstick, just in case Rah was on the receiving end of those shots.

As I took three timid steps toward the kitchen, Rah came out, brandishing a pizza pocket. He held it up so I could see.

"It was in the microwave."

I shake my head, and we both move towards the back of the apartment. Hopefully, AD has his situation under control.

When we made it to the back bedroom, at first, we didn't see bro. He heard our footsteps and called out to us.

"I'm in the bathroom."

We walked in. Dame was sitting on the toilet, pants down to his ankles, brains all over the toilet tank. AD caught him while he was taking a shit.

I looked at my watch. We'd already been in there a minute and a half.

"Time to move," I murmured.

At first, it's like he didn't hear me. AD just stared at Dame's lifeless body—until Rah snapped him out of it.

"AD! LET'S MOVE!"

Once he snapped out of it, we rushed out of there. Once outside, Rah looked up at the same apartment from earlier. The blinds were still open, and the light was still on.

"Let's go!" he urged.

We made it back to the Explorer, loaded up, and flew back home to the East.

***

Now, it was close to two-thirty in the morning. I'm posted up at my Uncle Lace's crib. My sister planned on bringing her lil boyfriend to the spot, and I ain't tryna be around for none of that. Lace is by far my favorite uncle. He's the uncle I first smoked weed with. He brought me to the strip club when I was sixteen, and let me pick a stripper. He helped me buy my first pistol. He was more like my big homie than my uncle.

He'd left around thirty minutes ago, talkin' 'bout he had to go pick up some lil freak. Knowing him, he'll probably pull back up with a bitch around my age.

Imagine my surprise when he came back to the crib—with Ms. Lavella!

As soon as they walked in, I could tell she was drunk out of her mind. She didn't even notice me sitting there in the living room. My uncle's slick ass positioned her so that her back was towards me. He began sucking on her ear, and kissing all on her neck. He stuck his hand under her dress and palmed her big ol' ass. I saw nothing but ass cheeks. I couldn't even tell if she had drawers on or not.

A part of me felt ashamed for watching my homeboy's momma like this—all exposed. Then the other part of me, the lower part, was excited.

My dick became hard as rock.

My uncle eyed me over her shoulder with a smile.

He took his middle finger, dug up in her panties, and pulled her G-string to the side. Her pussy popped out, and I groaned. My boxers began to stick from the precum oozing out the tip of my dick.

As if to torture me some more, he whispered in her ear.

She dropped to her knees—right there in the doorway.

My uncle allowed her to fish out his rod. With a devious smirk on his face, he pulled her head toward his crotch.

My homie Kay's mom began to gobble up my uncle's cock, right there in the living room. And I'm stuck in my seat, watching. Her dress was still bunched around her waist. Her ass cheeks jiggled each time she bobbed her head. I wanted so bad to take my dick out and jack off to the scene in front of me. Or maybe even join in. Bend her completely over and just ram my dick up in her.

D, you tripping. That's your nigga's T-Lady, I scolded myself.

Before temptation got the better of me, I hopped off the couch and ran into the guest room. My dick made an obvious tent in my shorts. When I looked back, right before I shut the bedroom door, I caught my uncle shaking his head, as if to say, *What a damn shame.*

Once I'm safely in the room, I whip my dick out and jack off. I came—not once, but twice—to the scene I'd just witnessed in the living room. I didn't know bro momma was freaking out like that. Not to mention, she was fine as fuck. Her pussy was fat as hell. I would never be able to look at her the same again.

I tried my best to shake the image out of my mind, but it was useless. I needed to ask her about Brodie. If he'd been getting the money I'd been giving Rah to send to him. I tried to get his info from Rah, but the nigga kept giving me the runaround. I gotta try and get it from Lavella in the morning.

After grabbing my sack out my stash, I twisted up some Za but only blew half a stick. Twenty minutes later, I was out like a light.

***

Next morning, I woke up and it's 11:15 a.m. I smelled breakfast cooking. I go into the kitchen, expecting to see Ms. Lavella getting to it. Instead, it was my uncle. No shirt, basketball shorts, and penitentiary tattoos everywhere. To be forty-five years old, he still had it. Those eight years in the pen preserved him.

"You hungry?" he asked.

"Hell yeah. My stomach ain't growling, that bitch is howling. Where's, um—"

"She left early this morning. You know, the older ones have bidness to take care of. Kids to get ready for school, grandbabies to take to daycare . . . husbands to see off to work." He paused to stir the eggs. Then he continued, "I thought you was gon' try and get you some of the wet vet last night."

"Unc, I can't do my nigga like that. That's the homie Kay momma. That's the one I told you, took the lick for the squad."

My uncle nodded in complete understanding.

"Well, I could definitely respect and salute that. Damn . . . that doesn't mean I can't tap that ass, does it?"

"Shit, y'all grown. Both of y'all damn near twice my age. Do you."

I was about to leave well enough alone, but I had to ask.

"She got some good, or what?"

"What, do she? Boy, let me tell you. That woman . . ."

My uncle spent the next thirty minutes telling me about Ms. Lavella and all the freaky shit they'd done the night before.

"She got that pressure. Top five best shot of pussy I done ever had—and that's saying a lot."

I hated the fact I didn't get a chance to chop it up with her before she left. I guess I'll have to try and catch her when she's not occupied.

Danielle

"Come on, come on, come on." I stared at the pregnancy test, praying to the heavenly father that it came back negative. *One line, negative. Two lines—* My heart dropped when I saw that second line appear. "No. No. No. No. I can't be pregnant. Not now. I stare at the test, blinking my eyes rapidly. Trying to will the result to change. "Shit!" I screamed out.

I sat down on the toilet seat, trynna get my thoughts together. I need to tell Rashard. Even though I've fucked a couple niggas barebacked, he's the only one I let nut in me. He's got to be the father. I figured something was wrong, when the scent of mere bacon made me sick. I threw up everywhere.

This wasn't the first time I've been pregnant. Kay and I had a miscarriage. I aborted another, because I was cheating on Kay, and had gotten pregnant while he was in the County. I didn't know who the daddy was, and I wasn't 'bout to go through none of that.

So, now that I'm pregnant again, I don't want to go to the chop shop. There's no telling if I would ever be blessed to have another. My nerves were all over the place. I forced myself to get up and head into the bedroom.

I honestly don't know how Rah's gonna take it. On one hand, he plays that role like he's loving on a bitch, but I know, as soon as I pop up with a bun in the oven, he's liable to switch up. Start talking out the side of his neck. My hands trembled as I dialed his number.

"Hello?" He sounded like he was at a store or something. I heard somebody on an intercom, talking 'bout an emergency on aisle seven.

"Rah, we need to talk."

"Okay, so talk."

"I would rather do it in person. When can you come over?"

He paused. "Really, I'll be tied up all day long. Just tell me what you got to say right now," he insisted.

Over the phone is definitely not how I wanted to discuss this situation, but I needed to get it over with—while I have the nerve too.

"Okay, fine," I concede. "I'm pregnant."

There. It's out. No sugarcoating. No beating around the bush. Straight laced, no chase.

"Pr—pregnant? Okay, so who's your baby daddy? Do I know the nigga?"

I pulled the phone back and looked at it. *Nigga!*

"You tell me. How well do you know yourself?" I retorted.

"Myself?" He chuckled. "You can't be serious. D, you serious?"

"Nigga, you think I'm 'bout to call you and play on this phone? What type of bitch do you take me for?"

Now, this nigga had me heated.

"A'ight, D, chill. We ain't gotta go that way. You just surprised a nigga, that's all. Sooo, what you think 'bout doing? I know you ain't trynna keep it, is you?"

"Psshht. To be honest, I *am* trynna keep it. I'm scared if I lose another baby, I won't be able to have any more."

He sighed heavily into the phone.

"D, a nigga ain't trying to be no daddy. Plus, Kay's my nigga and—"

I know this nigga ain't just bring up Kay.

"Kay? Nigga, did you just bring up Kaydon's name? You and I both know you don't give a fuck 'bout Kay like that. Why you weren't thinking 'bout Kay when you were jumping up and down in my pussy? Or when you was fucking my throat, nutting all in my mouth? I'm willing to bet you ain't sent him a dollar or wrote him one sentence. If I didn't know any better, I'd say you set him up to take the fall, so you could get him out the way."

I want to hurt him. I can't do it physically, so I tried it with words.

"*Bitch!* What you just say?" Rah was seething, but I wasn't about to back down.

"Yeah, bitch nigga, tell the truth, shame the devil."

"Look out, you trash-ass thot. Don't act like you wasn't trynna eat a nigga dick off the bone every chance you got. Soon as I pull up, you'd throw that ass all in my lap. Yeah, Kay is my nigga, but I'm a dog that fucks dirty-ass bitches like you. But *you*—you was supposed to be his heart. His better half. You don't think I know how you rocking, Dee? Hmph. I know at least four different niggas that have been sliding on the regular. Now you trynna pull up on me talkin' that pregnant shit? *Bitch, eat my dick!*"

Click!

I flinched. The fuck nigga just hung up in my face. I'm so motherfucking mad, I damn near threw the phone across the room.

Niggas ain't shit!

I had to laugh. What did I expect? He's fucking his best friend's girl. I should have known he wasn't a stand-up guy. I hadn't even realized I started crying.

Damn, a bitch didn't want to do this on her own. For the first time in a long time, I thought about Kay. If it was him I told I was pregnant, he would've jumped for joy. Regret and guilt started to settle in. I didn't even give it a chance. Now, I wish I would have. At least he could have been there to help navigate me through life. Someone who knows the real me. Someone whose advice I know came from a genuine place.

I contemplated writing him for the first time since he'd been shipped to the pen. Then I realized—it was too late for all that. Anything I'd say now, he'd dismiss it. Even if he did write me back, our relationship would never be the same again.

The rest of the night, I spent mapping out my next set of moves. The only thing I was absolutely sure about: I was gonna keep the baby. Even if I had to raise him or her by myself. So be it.

Chapter 9

Rashard

I'm at the carwash off Wallisville, sittin' in the Charger, thumbin' through the Gram. I see a shadow slide past the front of the whip—look up, and it's a face I know too well.

"Wassup, KeedaWee? What you got goin', fam?"

With him, it could be anything. Today? Might be some fresh-ass J's. Tomorrow? Burners, phones, or some other flip. One thing 'bout KeedaWee—that nigga stay gettin' it. Straight hustler, no breaks.

Lil nigga stood like five-six, maybe one-forty-five soaking wet. Ain't look like much—but Wee showed the hood so much love, *you fuck with him, you gotta see everybody.* "Aww Rah, today's special is them Fits," he said, smirkin' with that country-ass drawl he stay talkin' in.

"What they look like?" I'm not one to mess with the counterfeits, but if them hoes looked official, I'd support my nigga's hustle.

Wee ran back to his black '92 Buick Park Avenue, popped the trunk, and started rummaging through it. Moments later, he returned. I popped the passenger door for him. He hopped in, smelling like Black & Milds.

"What you got, Wee?"

He produced a bread bag with a bundle of cash in it. I untied it, reached inside, and pulled out a rubber-banded stack. My eyebrows climbed in mild surprise. So far, the Fits looked great. I peeled off a hundred-dollar bill and inspected

110

it. Now, they looked better than great. I pulled a hundred out my pocket and held up both bills side by side. The only difference—the fake bill had a darker shade of green. Other than that, everything else was on point. The color scheme, the texture, everything!

"How much? What you doing on these?"

"Well, I got like eighty-five hundred in the bread bag. Just fuck with me on eight hundred, and that's you," Wee bargained.

"Bet!" I count out the eight hundred and hand it over to him. As Wee dabbed me up and hopped out my whip, I already knew who I was gonna hit with the Fits.

There's a nigga I met in the County one time, named Xavier. He was from Greenspoint, Imperial Valley. Xavier had caught a possession charge. His thing was pills—pharmaceuticals. I had a pistol case I'd gotten dropped down to unlawful carry of a firearm. We ended up getting out the County around the same time.

The whole time we were in there together, we were kicking it every day. We'd get our lil females to bring their homegirls up there to visit one another. Once we hit the blacktop, we linked up a few times. A couple trips to the club, but we were in two different lanes.

He was a hustler. Me? I'll take a nigga's ass down. Jack Boy! Of course, Xavier didn't know this. He thought I was a hustler myself. Why would I let the sheep know I'm a wolf?

I scrolled through my contacts, then dialed his number.

"Hello?" he answered.

"What's the word, my nigga?"

"Same shit. Getting to that bag. Where you been? I ain't heard from your ass in a minute. What you got going?"

"Same shit you on—bag chasing. Matter fact, that's why I'm calling you. You still in motion with the pills?"

"Always. Plus, I got some of that smoke. Straight Za, if you trynna fuck with that too."

"What's the ticket?"

"How many you trynna fuck with?"

"Give me a K of them Percs, and half a bow of that smoke."

Xavier paused for a second, doing the math in his head.

"Okay, this what I'll do for you. I'm finna bless your game. I'll give you the K pack of Percs, plus the half a bow, for seventy-five hundred."

I already knew the ticket would be around that much. Still, I had to play the role.

"That's a bet. I can do that," I finessed.

"When you trynna pull up?"

"Shit, I can head over there right now. You on the Valley?"

"Naw, naw. I'm over here on Ella. You know where the Polo Club's at?"

"Yeah, I know where you're at," I told him.

I jumped out my whip and popped my hood. While ending the conversation with Xavier, I reached beside my engine and grabbed my Glock 32.

"I'm on the way," I said before hanging up.

I thought about scooping up Demon but decided against it. I really didn't think Xavier was built like that anyway. At least, he wasn't in the County.

It took me thirty-three minutes to make it to Ella Blvd from the East. I made the left into Polo Club Apartments. I noticed niggas outside, draped in blue, sitting on the stairs. I fingered the trigger on my Glock, turned into an empty parking lot, and called Xavier.

"Hello?"

"Yeah, I'm out here."

"What you in?"

"Black SRT Charger, on twenty-fo's," I replied.

"I'm 'bout to be out there."

I wait. The whole time, checking my rearview and side mirrors for anything suspicious. I wasn't used to feeling like the possible prey. This could easily be a setup. They feel like I got close to eight grand on me. Easy money!

Just when I'm about to call Xavier again to see what's taking him so long, I see him approaching my car through my side mirror. I unlocked the door, thinking he was about to get in to complete the transaction. Instead, he approached the driver-side window. I rolled the window down for him.

"My bad, my nigga, my lil cousin just got locked up. I gotta shoot downtown to bond him out, but here you go though."

He handed me a grocery bag, taped up. The package is a lil bigger than an NFL football. I don't waste time inspecting it in front of him. Instead, I hand him the envelope with the money in it. I guess since I didn't inspect the dope in front of him, he extended the same trust by not counting the money in front of me.

His mistake!

"It's all good, I'll catch up with you this weekend. We can hit Bottoms Up, see what new hoes they got up there," I tell him, as I backed out of the parking spot and pulled out of the apartments.

As soon as I passed through the exit gate, I laughed. That shit was too easy! I knew one thing—when he did count that bread, he was gonna be pissed.

I turned onto Ella, and my face fell. It appeared to be a three-car accident close to the light. I tried to quickly reverse, but there was already a line of cars behind me. So now, I'm forced to wait it out. Unless I tried to make a U-turn into the oncoming lane. But if I do that, I'd have to go all the way around and that might—

Bocka! Bocka! Bocka!

"Oh shit!" I yelped.

My passenger window exploded. Bits of glass ricocheted off my face, nicking my flesh. I felt searing heat graze my temple. My head hits the driver-side door, as if I was sucker punched. My pistol slid off my lap. I scrambled to reach it, but the shots kept coming—

Bocka! Bocka! Bocka! Thunk! Thunk!

Shells penetrated the car's frame. My heart pounded out my ribcage. I turned the wheel heavily to the left and smashed on the gas. The car jerked out of traffic, but others were doing the same thing. So now, my exit route was congested also.

Bocka! Bocka!

The back windshield shattered.

"Shit. Fuck!"

Blood seeped into my eyes. My head's aching something serious. I veered into the grass and sidewalks, desperately trying to get away from the barrage of bullets. I was scared to sit all the way up. I drove with my eyes barely over the dashboard.

I cleared three or four cars before I jumped back on the main road. By then, I looked back and saw three blue-flag-wearing Crips, standing on the sidewalk. Pistols at their sides, still smoking hot.

Pride demanded I go back and let my gun bark. But my rational, more logical mind understood—that would have been the dumbest move in American history. I needed to get to the spot and dump the drugs off, as well as stash the pistol.

My eyes burned. Blood and sweat, impeding my vision. I pulled over in order to clean myself up. I flipped the visor down and noticed the right side of my face was covered in my blood.

Now that the adrenaline had worn off, my head felt like it was about to explode. Panic began to set in. My eyelids were getting heavy. I knew I wouldn't make it all the way to the East.

I called Demon, but he didn't pick up. Even though we'd just had that fight, I called Danielle. Luckily, she answered. I begged her to come get me. Once she promised she would, I sat there and waited on her.

I don't know when, or how it happened, but somehow I dozed off.

***

I woke up on a couch. Head aching, body sore. It took me a couple minutes to realize where I was at.

Danielle came out the kitchen with some herbal tea and some pain pills. I struggled to sit up. It felt like my head weighed a hundred pounds.

"Whoa, slow down, cowboy," she teased, as she handed me the pills and the tea. "Here, this should make you feel better."

I took the pills and swallowed them down with one gulp.

"My car?" I asked, throat scratched and parched.

"It's safe. I got my sister with me. She drove your car back here. I ain't gon' lie though—you got 'bout ten bullet holes in it. With a shattered back windshield, as well as your passenger window."

I wanted to ask her about the dope and guns, but she had read my mind.

"I got your work and your pistol in the room. It's safe, Rah. All you need to do is relax and get yourself better."

I exhaled, relieved I didn't lose what I almost died for.

"I'm not gonna ask you what happened. All I need to know is, is this gonna follow you here? Because I can't have that. Especially since my lil sister just came home yesterday."

"Naw, you good, D. On my word. They don't even know you exist," I replied honestly.

She seemed satisfied with that answer, got up, and headed back into the kitchen.

I barely took notice—she had on a pair of small, red, French-cut panties and a white and red *Hello Kitty* tee. As my dick began to stir, my head began to throb. I reached up and felt the bandages.

"What happened to my head?" I called out.

She poked her head out of the kitchen.

115

"You must have gotten grazed pretty bad. You were bleeding all over the place. Instead of penetrating, the bullet ricocheted off your skull. Your ass is lucky as hell," she chuckled.

"Well, thank you. I know you didn't have to come get a nigga, so thank you. I really appreciate it."

"Whatever, nigga, that shit wasn't free. When you get back right, you *will* break a bitch off," she said with a slight smile—but I know she was serious as a heart attack.

"You hungry?"

"Hell yeah!"

Just as I say that, the front door to her apartment opened up, and in walked her nineteen-year-old sister, Alison.

Now, Danielle is a bad bitch. But knowing her mileage diminishes her beauty, just a bit. Alison, on the other hand, was pure as the driven snow.

Five-foot-ten, a hundred and forty-eight pounds. C cups and a perfect thirty-eight-inch ass. Alison had a *Straight Stunna* body. Her skin tone was a shade darker than her sister's.

Where Danielle is all about the streets and the niggas who run it, Alison is all about school—and the niggas who attended.

As a stand-out volleyball star, she went to college on a full academic scholarship. That's where she met her boyfriend, Chance—a sophomore basketball player.

"Oh!" She paused when she saw I was up. "Wassup? I'm glad to see you're alive, Rah."

I've been knowing Alison for as long as Kaydon and Danielle had been messing around. Back when she was a pimply-faced, awkward, skinny lil thing.

I've also watched her blossom into a beautiful, fine young woman.

"Yeah, I'm glad to be alive," I responded, playfully.

"Alison, did you remember to grab the bell pepper?" Danielle asked from the kitchen.

Alison rolled her eyes for my benefit.

"Of course. How could I forget? You only told me like six times."

"That's because you'd forget your own name if we didn't call you by it," Danielle retorted.

For some reason, anytime these two get around each other, they argue like cats and dogs.

As I watched them stand next to each other, I couldn't help but imagine what a threesome would feel like. *Who has the better pussy? Whose head game is superior? Who fucks the hardest?*

All these questions float in my mind, as I laid on the couch, trynna recover.

My phone vibrates.

It's a text message from Xavier:

We'll C U again.

I read the message and smiled.

I'll be waiting.

Kaydon

"We gotta hurry up. I just got a call on my radio. They want me at B-turn out."

Ms. Dean unbuckled her pants, reached inside her biker tights, and pulled out the pack.

This was the second time she'd dropped off for me. The first was a cell phone, so I could talk to her as much as I needed. Plus, I'd be able to move the money a lot easier. Now, she was dropping off straight work—sheets of K-2 and a zip of Ice.

"What you think they want?"

I doubt it could be about us. No one knows she's dropping off for me but my celly. She picked up on my concern.

"We good. My coworker went home sick. They need me to work two blocks. So, I won't really be able to sit still today," she told me, as she was tucking her shirt back in and buttoning up her pants.

"Oh, okay. I'll hit you up when you get off tonight then. That bread'll already be on your app."

She nodded, then bit her bottom lip. Mischief danced in her pupils. Dean reached for my dick, giving it a tight squeeze.

"Let me just taste it real quick."

"But I thought you just said they needed you at turnout?"

"They do. But I need to get a quick taste of that."

She peeled my waistband down and my heavy dick flopped out. Ms. Dean and I had been talking freaky to one another every night we been on the phone. Come to find out, she was a stone-cold freakazoid who just *loves* to eat that dick. Up until now, we hadn't had the opportunity to fuck around.

She squatted down in front of me, left hand on my right thigh, right hand gripping my piece. She shoveled the head of my cock into her mouth and actually moaned when the precum glazed her taste buds.

My toes curled in my *Reeboks*. Her mouth felt warm around my dick. I tilted my head back, closed my eyes, and pictured fucking a wet, warm pussy.

"OH ssshit . . . Damn!" I groaned as she bobbed her head at a rapid pace.

My low-hanging balls swung, tapping her on the chin like a prized boxer.

Ghlup—ghlup—ghlup.

Her spit trickled down my sack, running down my inner thighs. I'm actually trembling. My nuts began to boil.

"Fuck, fuck, fuck . . ." I chanted, as my dick spasmed. I squeezed on her shoulder, letting her know I'm 'bout to buss.

Ms. Dean pulled me all the way into her throat as my cum erupted from the tip of my dick—coating the back of her neck, sliding down her trachea, and filling her tummy up.

As I stood there shivering, she suckled lightly on the tip, until my balls were completely depleted. Reluctantly, she pulled back, allowing my piece to fall out of her mouth.

"Hmm hmm hmm. I knew you had a delicious dick," she said as she tucked me back in.

Dean stood up, reached in her back pocket, and brought out some napkins. After wiping her mouth dry, she pulled out and popped an *Altoid* mint before heading out the utility closet.

I waited about five minutes. Then, I made my move.

Soon as I get back to the block, I head straight upstairs to my cell. My celly was waiting on me. He popped the cell, and I passed him the pack. Then I head back to the dayroom, to let the workers on the other sections know—it was game time.

When the in-and-out came around, I went in. Me and my celly put together some packs for the hustlers on the team. After supplying the land, we did our thing and before we knew it, it was time for another drop.

Months went by. My celly and I had the whole unit on lock.

Through Ms. Dean, I was able to secure another set of legs—her homegirl, Ms. Truman. We had just about every lucrative drug you could think of circulating around the unit.

Even though Ms. Dean and I are supposed to be a *"couple,"* I started to notice Ms. Truman's flirtatious ways—the licking of the lips, the eyeing of the crotch, the sexual innuendos.

I *do* want to test-drive that pussy or head one time, but I was able to resist. I definitely didn't need anything fucking up my operation.

1:00 p.m. came. I sent the line down the run to my stash man to get my phone. When I got it back, I logged on to my page and saw I had a message in my DM from Claudia.

Her and I had been getting real close lately. In fact, sometimes Claudia would be the one grabbing the pack and meeting up with Ms. Dean or Ms. T.

I offered to pay her, but she would always say, *"You need it more than me. Save it for when you get out."*

I've been stacking like crazy. I read the message:

Bear_Claw69: *Hey big head. When u get on, get at me.*

I see her online light is still active.

I buss back: *Wassup. Can u FT?*

Instead of replying, my phone started silently ringing. Incoming video call. I answered. Claudia's face popped up.

In the background was a shower curtain. Only her face's on screen, so I couldn't really make out what's going on. But my curious mind wouldn't stop wondering.

"Heyy," she sang out, joyfully.

"Wassup, Claw?"

I gave her the nickname *Bear Claw*. Once I saw her pussy print in one of those pics, I told her she didn't have a camel toe—she had a bear claw. Since her name was pronounced *Claw-dea*, it fit.

"Well, I was just about to jump in the shower when I saw you in my DM."

"Yeah, I saw you had hit me earlier, so I was bussin' back. Is everything good?"

"Oh yeah, it's great. I talked to your lawyer. He said the private investigator had a chance to talk to one of the victims. Turns out, the victim is willing to sign an affidavit saying he wasn't completely truthful on the stand."

She saw my look of shock and relief and continued.

"Yeah. He said they saw you prior to the incident, but you had already left when they got robbed. But he stated emphatically—you were *not* one of the ones that robbed them."

A great weight was lifted off my shoulders. Finally, vindication. I trembled with excitement.

"So, what's the next step?"

"The lawyer said he has to file an application for a writ with the trial court. Then, he'll put a motion in for a hearing. If and when they grant it, you'll be bench-warranted back to the county."

A great big smile stretched across my face. In the years I've been locked up, this was the best news I'd ever received.

Claudia smiled.

"You're almost home, baby boy," she sang.

"Yeah, but it ain't over with yet," I commented.

Suddenly, Claudia turned her body. Her back was facing the bathroom mirror.

At the position the phone was in, I got a clear view of her backside.

Baby girl was naked as the day she was born. My voice stopped mid-sentence.

For the first time, I saw her body in all its glory. Her skin was smooth and without blemish. Her booty was fluffy and hung ever so slightly. Her pussy was so fat I could see it dangling from the back.

"What's wrong?" she asked slyly.

"I uh . . . I uh . . . Damn. No cap, Claw, you a bad bitch," I admit.

She blushed.

"Well, thank you. You're not so bad yourself."

She was about to add to that, but something caught her attention off-screen.

"Oh, I'm 'bout to jump in the shower, Harrell."

I guessed my brother must have knocked on the door. She mouthed, *"I gotta go, I'll come see you this weekend."* Then, the call disconnected.

I sat back and thought about everything we just talked about. I didn't want to get too excited, but I couldn't help it. Things were finally looking up.

Then I thought 'bout Claudia—and that back shot.

She had to have known I would see that, I told myself.

Yeah, that's my brother's wife, but the things she was doing for me had me feeling some type of way.

Because of her, I was able to do what I loved doing. Hustling!

Not only does she meet up with the legs, but she catches, holds, and moves all of my bread for me.

It's like she's my wife.

I shook the thought from my head and hit up Ms. Dean. Claudia had me worked up.

Imma have to have Ms. Dean eat this dick up tomorrow.

Chapter 10

Andrea

"Wassup. We going out tonight, or what?" I asked Danielle. It'd been weeks since we'd fucked around with Jack and them. Once again, I needed to let loose.

"Naw, girl, not tonight. I got my lil sister staying with me. I told her I'd take her to pick up her lil boyfriend from the airport. Apparently, both of them planned on staying with me for the summer."

Danielle didn't sound too pleased about that.

"Okay, girl. I guess I'll see what Tiara's talking 'bout then."

We disconnected. I searched through my contacts. As I scrolled down my list, I spot Kelly's name—my coworker. *Hmmph.* She had always been begging me to go out with her. *Fuck it!*

I dialed her number up.

"Hello?"

She sounded as if she was riding in a car. There was a lot of blowback from the wind.

"Hey, girl. Can you hear me?"

"Huh? Wait, hold up."

Seconds later, the wind dissipated, and she hopped back on the phone.

"Hello?"

"Yeah. Wassup? What you got going?"

"I just left the gym, and I'm headed home. Why, what's good?"

"Do you got plans for tonight?" I asked.

"Uh, not really."

"Are you trynna go out? Club Heat has a lingerie party. Best dressed gets a thousand dollars."

"Oh, okay. What time?"

"The club opens at ten. We gone pull up around eleven-thirty-ish."

"Sure. In that case, I'm about to make a detour. Need to go pick up something to wear," she said.

I told her I'm about to do the same thing, then we hung up.

I really don't think the white girl has any flavor, but she might surprise me, so I don't do no half-steppin'.

I swung by *Victoria's Secret* and grabbed me something to shut the party down. I was definitely trying to leave out of there with the thousand-dollar prize.

By the time ten o'clock rolled around, I was laced up, oiled up, and ready to go.

We agreed I would drive, since it was my idea. That meant Kelly could get as lit as she wanted to. I threw a coat over my outfit and headed out the door.

Twenty-three minutes later, I arrived at her crib.

After honking the horn, she stepped out with her black coat on. I couldn't see her outfit, but I took note of her heels—six inches, with pink fur around the toe. *Cute,* I admit to myself.

She hopped in smelling like apple cinnamon. Her lips, glazed cotton candy pink. Her face beat to perfection. The bitch is looking like Kim K's little cousin or something.

"Oh shit, girl. You definitely clean up nice," I complimented.

Seeing her at work, I would've never guessed she'd be able to transform into such a startling beauty.

"You're not so bad yourself."

124

She doesn't have to tell me that. I know I'm shutting it down.

"Wait till you see what I'm rocking," I teased.

We both agreed we wouldn't reveal our outfits until we got inside the club. Just seeing her shoes had me intrigued.

We arrived at the club, and the parking lot was already packed. Women got in free if they had on lingerie, but the men had to pay a hundred to get in.

I parked, and we hopped out. We both flashed the doorman our outfits, so he could allow us entry.

Soon as we stepped foot in the club, we knew the night would be memorable. The atmosphere was electric.

Women and men walked around barely dressed. They came in all shapes and sizes.

Kelly shed her coat first. She was rocking a pink teddy with fur trim. Her titties were sitting up—nice and perky. Nipples already at attention. And by the looks of it, they were larger than normal.

Her pink lace thong had a small patch of fur on the crotch area.

She went for the classy-but-sexy look.

Her mistake.

I allowed my coat to fall off my shoulders.

I was rocking a cherry red, silk, crotchless bodysuit. My D-cups were up and at it. My stomach was out. Flat. Traces of a six-pack, evident.

My fat, bald pussy was out on display. A red, open G-string covered my clit. My chunky sex lips hung free for the world to see.

My four-inch heels, aligned with red leather.

As we stood there, freshly revealed, men stopped and stared, nodding their approval.

We decided to split up and meet back at the bar around 1:00 a.m. The DJ said they would announce the winner of the contest at 1:45 a.m.

I knew I couldn't drink too much, but that didn't stop me from indulging in a lil cocaine.

I danced the night away.

Every now and then, I would allow a finger up my pussy, or I would slip my hands into someone's boxer briefs and grip their dicks while we danced.

By the time it came to announce the winner, Kelly and I stood side by side.

Well, really *I* stood. She more like, wobbled and staggered in place.

When they announced the winner, I literally jumped for joy.

I ran onstage to accept the prize and allowed the manager to squeeze my ass while he gave me a tight, seductive hug.

"I see you, girl," he whispered in my ear.

I felt his dick through his *Armani* slacks. Dude was definitely packing something nice.

I did a quick shimmy, then pranced my ass off stage.

I returned to where Kelly was and immediately knew something was wrong.

She was cussing up a storm, but due to the noise level of the club, I doubted whoever she was talking to could hear her.

"What the fuck, Tee? You want me to sit up in the house all day, wait on your ass to come home when you feel like it?" she yelled, slurring in the process.

"What? I can't hear you. Hello? Yeah, I'm here, but I can't hear you."

I assumed she was talking to her boyfriend. I tapped her on the shoulder and mouthed, *"Let's go outside."*

She nodded, then followed me out.

Once we stepped out of the club, the cool night air hit my face. I immediately felt euphoric.

My clit began to tingle. I subconsciously looked around to see if I could scrape up some dick for the night.

"I'm not trynna hear that shit, nigga!"

I snapped my head around.

Hearing her say the word *nigga* was a cultural shock to me. I'd been working with her for eight months, and I'd never heard her say the word.

I grit my teeth and let it pass.

I hope she don't think, just because she fucks Black dick, sucks Black dick, and eats Black babies, that she's miraculously Black.

"Whatever, Tee. I don't know. Psshht. Hold on."

She put her phone on speaker as we sat in the car.

"Hello?"

A deep, sultry voice called out.

My ears instantly perked up. I'm not sure what's really going on, but the look Kelly gave me, I assumed I'm supposed to be answering back.

"Uhh, hello?"

"Say, where y'all at right now? I'm tryna meet up so she could hop in the car with me."

"You know where Club Heat at?" I asked.

"Yeah, but ain't y'all headed back to the East?"

"Well, I was trynna go get me something to eat first, but I could meet you halfway."

It sounded as if he was mulling it over.

"A'ight. Meet me on I-10 and Waco Drive. In the *Frenchy's* parking lot."

Kelly took the phone and began to talk into it.

"Okay. You feel better now? You always try—" *Click.* He hung up in her face.

"Uggghh. That muthafucka makes me so sick sometimes. I swear, if the dick wasn't so fucking good, I would have been left his ass."

My ears *and* pussy perk up at the mention of some good cock.

My mind flashes back to the pics I saw on her phone. A couple of them were close-ups. He had a long, thick, nutmeg-colored dick. It had to be him.

The way he's acting, she would've never been able to have no other nigga's pics in her phone.

I need to find a way to push up on dude without being noticeable. *Think, think, think.*

I heard a *clunk* as Kelly dropped her phone into the cup holder. Then it hit me.

As we turned into the parking lot, Tee Lee's already standing outside of his black *BMW 750Li*, waiting on us. Fuming.

I took his appearance in—six foot, one inch, two hundred-plus pounds, with a nice solid build. I could tell from his skin tone, that was definitely pictures of his dick in her phone.

He didn't wait until the car fully stopped before he approached the passenger-side door, yanking it open.

He was 'bout to go ham on Kelly, but when he saw me, it gave him pause.

I don't know if it was the fact I was a potential witness, or that my legs were gapped open—coochie lips sitting out, engorged with blood from my arousal.

Whatever the reason, he went from a hundred to sixty.

"Come on," he growled at Kelly, while holding the door open.

I guess she was taking too long—he snatched her by the back of the neck and pulled her out of the car.

"Muthafucka, get your hands off me," she protested. But due to her drunken state, it came out as a whine.

My pussy wouldn't stop dripping. That rough shit gets me going every time.

I need my man to snatch me up and hold me down while he fucks some sense into me. If a nigga lets me run over him, when it's time for us to have sex, my coochie won't even get wet.

I watched as he yanked the passenger door on the Beamer open, then tossed her inside like a bag of dirty laundry.

As Tee Lee headed back over to his driver side, him and I locked eyes.

I knew then—he was *mine.*

I just had to reel him in.

As they pulled off, I hurriedly reached under my seat, where I discreetly stashed Kelly's phone.

I knew her screen code from me just being nosey.

Once I got in, I quickly went to her contacts and found his number under *Hubby.*

I programmed the number in my phone, then just to be nosey some more, I sifted through her video/photo gallery.

A video of her giving head—trynna tackle that big, bad muthafucka—popped up.

I gotta keep it a hot one hundred . . . that white girl could eat some dick.

Just as I was 'bout to click on the next video, the phone rang. The caller ID said: *Hubby.*

I debated on whether or not to answer.

I didn't want to expose the fact I knew her code, so I allowed it to ring.

Obviously, they'd realized Kelly had left her phone.

I figured they'd be making a U-turn, so I stayed rooted.

Sure enough, moments later, the black Beamer pulled back up into the parking lot.

I closed out the apps and sat the phone on the passenger seat.

I thought Kelly would've been the one to get out—but instead, it was Tee Lee.

His long legs took no time getting to my car.

I rolled the window down, picked the phone up, and presented it to him.

"I knew you would be back, so I stayed put," I told him, making sure to put the emphasis where it needed to be.

He grabbed the phone, but his eyes were locked between my legs.

I smirked.

"Yeah, if her head wasn't screwed on, she would leave that muthafucka. Sometimes, she acts like she has."

"Don't be too hard on her. Good dick will make the best of us lose our minds sometimes," I said, *bodily.*

He hit me with a nervous chuckle. He's probably never met a chick who was so aggressive and straight-forward.

He realized he'd been at the car too long. He looked back—Kelly was giving him the stink eye.

"A'ight, appreciate it." He held up the phone for her benefit.

I fucked him up when I said, *"Be expecting my call."*

With a subtle nod and a small smile, he walked back to his car.

As I merged back onto I-10, I grabbed my phone to see what my baby daddy was doing.

After everything that went down, I needed my back beat in.

Soon, I'll get to see what type of stroke game Tee Lee's working with.

If he's like Kelly said he is, I'll put him in rotation.

She'd have to learn—*Black dick comes wit' Black problems.*

And the biggest problem is a pretty face, fat ass, pink pussy Black bitch getting at her man.

Danielle

Finally, it's 5:30 p.m.—quitting time. I head to the back to clock out. Carl was sitting at his desk doing paperwork. Flashbacks of when he had me perched upon that same desk, feeding on my box, flooded my mind. I thought once he got a taste of this hundred percent peach juice, he'd get all thirsty on me. Instead, it was as if it never happened. Which, by the way, is cool with me. I guess he just wanted to get it out of his system.

Once I'm clocked out, I practically run outside and jump in my Camry. Just those couple of feet had me sweating. Jesus, it's hot! I turned the A/C on full blast and made my way home. Even though I'd been around BBQ all day, my body wouldn't allow me to eat it. Yet, I'm hungry enough to eat a hostage. I hoped Alison fixed something to eat.

Ever since we went and picked up her boyfriend, Chance, from the airport, it was like the bitch had gotten lazy. All she wanted to do was lay around and take dick all day. I understand you missed the nigga, but damn!

I pulled up to the apartment complex. Niggas with obvious guns tucked inside their waistbands stood around loitering. I really needed to move—especially with a baby on the way. I subconsciously looked down at my baby bump. I'm ten weeks plus now, and starting to show. This by far is the furthest I've ever been in a pregnancy. And this baby is already kicking my ass.

My hormones are all over the place. My appetite is sporadic. My body doesn't know if it wants to be hot or cold. I parked, then hopped out. The sun is still out beaming. I shade my eyes with my hand as I made my way to my apartment.

I reached into my purse and dug my keys out. I unlocked the door and stepped in. As soon as I crossed the threshold, my face fell into a frown. Laid, cuddled up under a blanket, was my sister and her boyfriend. My sense of smell was heightened. The scent of sex filled my nostrils. The living room was a mess. Clothes were sprawled out everywhere. An empty box of Popeyes chicken sat on the coffee table.

"Oh, hey, Danielle," Alison had the nerve to fix her lips and tell me.

I don't trust myself to say anything, so I just grunt a reply, then head into the bedroom. I was in desperate need of a shower. My sticky skin made me feel irritated.

Once I'd stripped down, I stepped inside the bathroom and saw panties dangling everywhere. On the shower rod. On the edge of the tub. I took a few deep breaths to compose myself. I tried to look at the bright side—they're clean, newly washed, just hanging out to dry. I collected them, then placed them on the outer rim of the laundry basket.

I'd hoped the shower would have soothed me. It did for a moment. Until I dried, dressed, and headed to the kitchen to fix something to eat. When I saw the sink full of dirty dishes, I lost it.

"Alison, what the fuck is wrong with you?" I screamed. Now that the knob had been adjusted, it would be hard to scale back my anger.

She got off the couch in nothing but a pair of yellow panties and a white wife beater.

"What's wrong?" she asked, confused.

"What's wrong? Bitch, look at these dishes. Look at this apartment. You weren't raised like this. What the fuck is wrong with you?" I know how she was raised, because I raised her.

Our mom died when I was sixteen years old. Alison was only six at the time. Dad tried to work to provide, but when he got laid off, he went back to what he knew—the streets. He ended up hitting a jewelry store, and one of the niggas who was with him told. Some old nigga named Curtis.

For the last eight years I had been raising Alison. I was so proud when she got the scholarship to play volleyball out of state. Now, she had some in-house dick, and she acted like she done lost her fucking mind.

"Come on, Danielle, it's not that serious," she claimed. "I'll clean the dishes in a lil bit, soon as I get done watching the movie."

"Naw, you 'bout to bring your ass in here and clean these muthafuckas right now." I wasn't playing with her ass. Not one bit.

I guess her lil feelings were hurt, or she was embarrassed because her lil boyfriend was there. She tried to call herself studding up.

"I said I'll do it when I'm done watching the movie, and don't talk to me like I'm some lil kid," she argued.

"Bitch, this is my motherfucking crib. I'll talk to whoever I want, however I want. On top of that, you acting like a lil girl who just got her first taste of some good dick. God damn. You got my shit looking like a pig sty. If I was him, I wouldn't want to stick my dick in no bitch that lived like this!"

That must have done it, because the next thing that came out her mouth was, "Fuck you. At least I got a man. I've been watching niggas run up in your blown-out pussy since I was eleven years old."

WHAP!

I slapped fire from her ass. She stumbled back in shock, then went on the attack. I'm not a punk bitch, and I sure didn't raise Alison to be one. So, if she couldn't do shit else, she could fight.

We exchanged blow for blow. Nothing pretty, just trying our best to hurt each other. I caught her in her lip. It split and began to bleed. She caught me in my left eye. I saw stars and felt it slightly begin to close. Still, we continued to brawl.

Finally, Chance grabbed Alison by the waist and restrained her.

"Alison, you're tripping. She's pregnant."

"Fuck that bitch, let me go!" she screamed, as she withered and twisted in his grasp.

I've never claimed to be a fair fighter. While Chance had her hemmed up, I ran over and got me a couple of good ones in.

WHAP — WHAP!

"Come on, Danielle, now you tripping, man," Chance admonished me.

Alison started going crazy, trying to get at me.

"I'm finna kill you, bitch. Chance, let me the fuck go. This bitch got me fucked up. Let me go!"

"You ungrateful lil hoe, get the fuck out of my house!" I yelled.

That calmed her all the way down. Since she was a kid, that was a promise I always made to her. No matter what, I'd never kick her out. Since we didn't really have any close relatives, we were all we had. If we ever turned our backs on each other, we'd have nowhere else to go. For me to kick her out was like the ultimate betrayal to her. It meant I didn't give a damn about her.

Alison just stood there—chest heaving, lip busted. The look on her face was of pure hurt, less anger. She waited for me to take it back. When I didn't, she went and threw on some shorts, grabbed a bag of clothes, some hygiene, and prepared to leave.

"Chance, you don't have to leave. I know you ain't from around here and don't have nowhere else to go," I told him.

I thought Alison was going to have a problem with that, but surprisingly she seemed relieved. Of course Chance tried to follow her, no doubt thinking it was the manly thing to do. Alison unselfishly convinced him to stay.

"No, Chance. Stay here. I can probably crash at one of my home girls from school. I need to make sure you have a roof over your head. I'll call you and let you know where I'm at," she said, as she walked out the apartment.

Chance stood there staring at the door for a half a minute before turning around. Without so much as a word, he began to clean up the mess Alison and I made. I watched him for a few minutes before deciding to help.

Once we were done, he took the trash out, and I washed the dishes. I retired to my bedroom and fell fast asleep. My whole body ached, and I knew I would be sore the next day.

What he was doing in the living room was his business. I know what we were both thinking though.

I wonder what Alison is doing right now.

Chapter 11

Rashard

I'm slidin' down Uvalde, fresh out the car wash. After that lil bullshit with that weak-ass nigga Xavier and his Crip homies, I had to get my baby back right. My old school—Link basket—always gon' be my favorite toy, but my Charger? That's my daily workhorse, all-purpose whip. Soon as I got the windows fixed, frame primed and patched up, and threw some new feet on her (the old rims got fucked up when I was tryna shake the spot), I was out like sixty-five hunnid. And that was a muthafuckin deal!

Good thing is, that work I jacked off that nigga covered all that shit—and then some. But now I'm fiendin' for another lick. Niggas love talkin' down on jack boys like we the scum of the streets. Man, fuck that. This shit a jungle—straight predator and prey. You don't see nobody cryin' when a lion snatch a gazelle to feed her cubs, right? So why the fuck you pressed when I do the same?

Anyway, I'm slidin' down the U when I peep this tall-ass shawty with a mean ass walk, struttin' down the side of the road. She had a backpack on, and by the way she was steppin', I could tell shorty wasn't in no good mood. But them red coochie cutters? Had me damn near slammin' the brakes. That ass was sittin', fat and disrespectful. I damn near hit the horn on reflex—*Beep—Beep.*

She turned at me with a frown. No doubt, about to cuss me out and tell me to get the fuck on. When she saw who I was, she softened up. When I saw who *she* was, my eyebrows climbed and my lips curled into a smile. "Girl, where you going, and what you doing walking?" As I asked, she was already opening the passenger side door.

Alison hopped in, with great exhalation. "Pssht. Danielle was tripping. Long story short, we got into it, she kicked me out."

"But, I thought your boyfriend Lance was over there too."

"Chance. His name is Chance," she corrected me, but I knew damn well what his name was. "I told him to stay there. I didn't want both of us on the streets."

"Wait a minute. On the streets? What you mean, on the streets?" You don't have nowhere else to go?" She looked out the window, too ashamed to answer. A devilish idea popped into my head. "Look, Alison, I'm not 'bout to let you be on the streets. You can come crash at my spot. I'll sleep on the couch. You can sleep on the bed. I'm pretty sure, your sister will calm down and let you come back home in a couple days. All I ask is this, do not tell anyone you're staying with me. If they ask who you're staying with, just tell them a female friend of yours."

A great big sigh of relief, eased passed her lips. Then quickly, she adds, "I don't have any money. So I can't pay you rent or anything."

"Girl, you're good. You're practically family," I told her. She seemed pleased with that.

"Thank you," she said, sincerely. We rode the rest of the way, in silence.

***

Two days after I picked up Alison, I'm at the spot with a couple of my lil niggas from the nine block (Homestead). I'm one of them type of niggas; I keep associates in every notorious hood in the city. That's what makes my stamp official. A couple of my lil homies from around the way came and stopped by to kick it. They'd been messing with some females from the East, and wanted the scoop on them, checking their background, to see if they were on the up and up.

We sat around, smoking and drinking on some Cognac. About twenty minutes after they got there, Alison came out of the room in some booty shorts, and a college basketball shirt. *That must be her boyfriend's,* I thought to myself, as all three of us were captivated by her body. "Were we making too much noise?" I asked, as she headed into the kitchen.

She turned with a sly smile. "Oh no. I didn't even know y'all were all in here," she claimed. *Yeah, right.*

Lil Mexico couldn't keep his eyes off her. "Damn, momma, you wanna come have a drink with us or what?"

I hurriedly interjected, knowing what her response would be. "Naw, she can't drink. She's still a baby. She ain't even twenty yet," I clowned.

Alison frowned her face up. "Boy, stop. I've been drinking since I was fifteen," she claimed.

My lil homie Tyson puts his two cents in. "This ain't no MD 20/20. This that grown and sexy right here," he said, while holding up his cup. She looked at me defiantly. I threw my hands up in mock surrender.

She grabbed a glass out the kitchen, and we poured her ass a stiff shot. She sat down on the couch next to me. "The first one has to go to the head," I told her.

Her eyes got big. "The whole shot?"

"Yes, the whole shot. That's what big girls do," I chide. We watched eagerly as she steadied her nerves. She tilted her head back, pinched her nose and with three gulps, finished the glass.

"Aww! Ssssshit," she hissed as she slammed the glass down. Her eyes began to tear up. She fanned herself with her right hand. Her thighs opened and closed, as the liquor coursed through her body. I don't give her no reprieve. I tilt the bottle over and give her another shot. After her second glass, Alison was already blitzed out of her mind.

She hadn't realized her shorts had rode up her pussy crack. We could clearly see the outline of her clit. As she sat with her legs gapped open, my lil homies were giving me all types of looks. They wanted to take her ass down. *Fuck her brains out.*

I shook my head. "Not while she's drunk like this," I whispered to Lil Mexico, when we both made our way to the kitchen.

"Come on, Rah, you know the lil bitch a freak. If not, she wouldn't have come out with the lil bitty ass shorts, with her pussy all out."

"You might be right. She may be a freak, but we not 'bout to toss her up while she's lit like that. Catch that bitch tomorrow, while she's sober," I told him. "Test your game. You act like you wanna cheat code or something." I poked at his pride.

"Cheat code. Mexico don't need no bitch fucked up, to get in her drawers," he boasted.

"Okay. Well, pull back up tomorrow when the bitch is sober and see where your game is at." Reluctantly, he agreed. We headed back into the living room.

Ten minutes later, I saw Alison could barely stay awake. I took her into the room, laid her down and headed back into the living room with the lil homies. We kicked it for another fifteen minutes. When they saw I wasn't about to let them buss her up, they caught ghost.

After I locked the door behind them, I stripped down to my boxers and made my way into the bedroom. Truth is, I didn't want *them* niggas to get a piece of the bitch's pussy just yet. I needed to be the first. I'm a jack boy. I *live* by the cheat code.

I twisted the knob, then pushed the door open. Alison was facedown, splayed out on the bed. *Knocked out!* I crept up on her, climbed aboard, then nibbled on her ear first. She stirred. "Chance?" she called out. I kissed her on her neck in reply. She moaned. I lifted the back of her shirt, and licked up and down her spine. She began to fidget.

Sitting back, I hooked my fingers into her waistband and peeled her shorts off her wide hips. Slow at first. But then I figured, why take the time? I yanked down, and Alison subconsciously adjusted herself, to allow me to remove her shorts the rest of the way.

Once her boy shorts hit the ground, I stared at her. Ass sitting up perfectly. Pussy popping out like a 3D picture. I don't bother with her shirt; she could keep her boyfriend's shirt on for all I care.

I slipped out my boxers, and pushed her legs apart. I needed room to work. "Eat that pussy baby," she called out, groggily. I spread her cheeks apart. The tip of my nose, resting in the center of her rosebud. My tongue dipped into the mouth of her pussy. Her juices tasted sweet and tangy. I lapped it up, caressing the insides of her pussy lips with my thick tongue. She moaned, "Chance baby. It feels sssoooo good."

I worked on her twat for a few more minutes, but my dick needed to get wet. I climbed aboard, gripping my piece at the base and placing it at her opening. I dipped the tip in and let her heat scorch my dick head before I slammed it home.

"Agggghhh ssshit!" she cried out, as I hit the bottom of her pussy. Balls deep. I grabbed the back of her neck, while working my hips. Her snatch is soaking, sloppy wet. "Oooh shit. This dick. This dick is too big. Fuck!"

I dug in, growled and gave her the bidness. Her booty cheeks wobbled and shook, as I gutted her like fish. "Oh fuck. Oh fuck. I'm cumming. Im cummmiinnnggg. Ssssshit!" Alison screamed into the mattress, as her first orgasm demolished her. Her walls constructed around my shaft, like the mouth of a Boa Constrictor. I used the crux of my feet to spread her legs apart.

Now, I could really dig in. With her face stuffed into the mattress, legs cocked open, there's nothing stopping me from beating her box loose. *Squelch—Squelch.*

"Huh. Huh. Huh. Huh." She panted, as I continued to carve up her inside. "Oh fuuuckkkk. I'm cumming again," she screamed. Her whole body convulsed. A warm stream of liquid shot out the back of her pussy.

Her teeth chattered, like it was freezing cold. I tried to hold on, but her young pussy was just too good. Wet, hot, tight and fresh. My nuts began to boil. Before I could blink, my balls bussed. "Aggghh ssssit," I groaned as I nut all up in Alison's pussy. Filling her up to capacity.

I collapsed on top of her, and stayed there. Eyes closed, she smiled. "That was the best ever baby," she whispered. Seconds later, she was back asleep, snoring lightly. I slipped out of her pussy. The minute I uncorked, streams of thick, white cum, poured from her gaping cunt. I found my boxers, slipped them on and headed to the shower.

***

The next morning, I awoke to the smell of breakfast being cooked. I sat up and saw Alison, busy in the kitchen— standing over the stove in a baby tee and a pair of boy shorts. I thought for sure she would've woken up on some more shit. Instead, she was as jolly as can be. When she noticed me staring, she smiled even brighter.

"Hey, Rah. You hungry?"

"Hell yeah," I croaked.

"Well, breakfast will be ready shortly," she said.

I go ahead and wake all the way up. I snatched the blanket off and stood up. Alison stared at my morning wood. When I caught her, she quickly averted her eyes. I smirked before I made my way into the bathroom.

After pissing, washing my face, and brushing my teeth, I head back into the living room. My plate was ready and sitting on the coffee table, along with a glass of fruit juice.

"What's all this?" I asked.

She bit her bottom lip. "For everything. For the hospitality. For looking out for me. You didn't have to do any of that. So this is my way of saying thank you."

To be honest, she had me perplexed. I didn't know if she had some type of angle or what. *Does she remember the beating I put on her pussy last night?*

If she did, she was intent on not saying anything 'bout it. To be honest, I wish she would say something. Anything. But she didn't. I checked the time. It's already 12:18 p.m. I needed to get going. I had a couple licks I had to scope out.

After finishing up my plate, I'm 'bout to get up and put it away in the sink, but Alison wouldn't have none of that.

"I got it, Rah," she told me, scooping up the tray.

I'm left looking at her backside, trynna figure out what the hell was going on.

Twenty minutes later, I'm dressed and out the door. *Damn, that lil bitch got some grade A pussy. A nigga gon' have to find a way to tap that on the regular,* I told myself, as I jumped in my Charger, cranked the engine up, and ventured into the concrete jungle.

Demon

The day was Wednesday. 1:00 p.m. That means I need to hit the gym. I usually go with AD, but ever since that situation, Brody been ducked off on some reclusive shit. I don't blame him though. Ain't no telling who Dame told that he'd clipped AD. So once he was found dead, two plus two ain't never been hard to add.

So, I'm headed to work out one deep. I would've seen if Rah wanted to go, but ever since the incident with the homie's girl, I've been distancing myself from him. Hitting licks, getting a bag is one thing, but just linking up to kick it? I'll pass. The crazy thing is, them niggas been locked in with each other their whole lives. If he'd do Kay like that, I could only imagine what he'd do to me.

I found a spot to park and hopped out of the car. The fitness center wasn't too crowded, so I was able to get on any machine I wanted. I noticed a female walk in that looked real familiar. I know her from somewhere. I had to catch myself—I didn't wanna keep staring at her like some perv. I guess she was thinking the same thing, because she eventually approached me.

"Excuse me, I don't mean to bother you, but would you happen to know a man by the name of Kaydon . . . Kaydon Snow?"

As soon as she said his name, it clicked. Recognition set in. *Keeda!*

"Yeah, that's my bro. Keeda, right?"

She lit up at the fact I knew who she was. To her, that meant she mattered in the homie's life—if his patnas knew her on sight.

"That's me. How has he been?"

I felt sudden guilt, knowing I didn't know the answer to the question. I hadn't spoken to bro myself in almost two years.

I couldn't tell her that, so I lied. "Shit, he's doing well. Keeping his head up and his chest out."

"That's good, that's good. Umm, I've tried to look him up on the site, but I must be doing something wrong, because I can't find him. I know his name is right, but I must have his birthday wrong or something."

The way she said it, it was like she was waiting on me to furnish her the information.

I didn't want to admit that I couldn't help her. "Check it, I got bro info at the crib. If you give me your info, or I give you mine, I could grab it later on and give it to you over the phone."

"Sure."

I pulled my phone out and we exchanged information. As I watched her walk away, I couldn't help but admire her body. Keeda wasn't the prettiest chick a nigga ever saw, but she sure wasn't the ugliest. Her body though? A ten. Nine point five at the least. Perfect washboard abs, toned up everything. Legs, thighs, ass—everything.

As she worked out, I eyed her through my peripheral. I could see why her body looked the way it did—she went hard as hell on the workout. Now, she was checking me out also. You know a nigga had to flex. By the time I was done, I knew I would be sore as hell in the morning.

Afterwards, I hit the showers, then went home. On my way there, I got a text message: *U feel like eating?*

I respond: *Sure. Y not.*

Moments later, my phone rung and I answered. Keeda and I agreed to meet at Chili's. We spent a few hours laughing and talking shit while we ate. The chemistry between us was amazing.

To be honest, I don't know how it happened, but thirty minutes after we got done eating, Keeda was laid on her back, head hanging off the side of the bed, as I fed her my dick. First, slowly. Then, I began to pick up a rhythm— fucking her throat with long, powerful strokes. *Awka— awka—awka!*

I reached forward, grabbed her titties, and twerked her nipples. Her legs peeled apart. Her pussy lips, slick and shiny. I stepped back and allowed my dick to fall out of her mouth.

"Stand up!" I told her.

Keeda hopped off the bed and stood in front of me, waiting for instructions.

"Turn around."

She committed a hundred-and-eighty-degree turn and assumed the position. I stepped back and admired how perfect her pussy looked from the back.

SMACK!

Her right ass cheek rippled, but it was firm, from her intense workout. I slid my middle finger up and down her slit. It came away slimy. I tasted her essence. *Perfect.*

I stepped to the plate, lined up, and with a great push, buried myself to the hilt.

"Ohhh, sshhitt!" she hissed, as I began to saw into her.

The rest of the afternoon was spent fucking each other's brains out. I didn't make it back to my sister's crib until late night, early morning. Now that I think about it, Keeda didn't even remember to ask for Kaydon's info. And add to that, I forgot to remind her.

AD

"Ten Toes Bonding Company, how can I help you?"

I recognized the voice. "Stephanie, is Big Ced in?"

"No, he's not. But who's this? Maybe I can help you."

"This is Allen. Allen Davin. I'm trynna see if I got any warrants."

"Oh, hey, AD. I don't think so. I know you've been calling every day, so I made it a habit to check, even if we haven't heard from you yet. Hold on, let me look real quick."

I hear computer keys clicking. "Uhhm . . . let's see," she murmured to herself. "Nope, still nothing. You're good."

I hadn't even realized I'd been holding my breath. "Appreciate it, Steph." Ever since we took care of Dame, I've been on pins and needles. I didn't know who he'd told about the robbery. Plus, Demon kept pushing for me to spank Kiera.

"No loose ends," he'd said.

"I can understand that, but Kiera is about as solid as they come," I responded.

But now, as the weeks go by, I can't help but ask myself: Did I make a mistake by letting her live?

I got out of bed and hopped my ass in the shower. For the last three weeks, I've been shacked up with this old-school smoker from my hood I'd been knowing most of my life, named Tink.

Tink used to be one of those sack-chasing females who all the dope boys wanted a piece of. She was unfortunate to have been a teenager in the late eighties, early nineties. Crack was the "it" drug at the time, and she was smoking boatloads of it.

Now, she was a former shell of herself. Five feet, five inches. Saggy titties, ashy skin, with a row of teeth missing—Tink couldn't buy a man's attention. Still, she had a lot of love for me.

When I used to run from the laws, she would let me hide out at her crib. I remember when I was fourteen, I'd gotten hit on the dice for eight hundred dollars. It was all I had to my name.

Tink found out, left, and three days later she pulled back up with three hundred dollars—crumbled-up tens, fives, and twenties.

"Here, get back on your feet. And never gamble what you can't afford to lose."

Since that day, I never have. Whenever she needed a lil help, I made sure I was there for her. When I showed up at her doorstep, pleading for a place to lay low, she didn't hesitate.

I jumped out of the shower, got dressed, and was headed out the door. Tink was in the living room, eyes glued to the TV, watching her stories.

"I'll be back," I said over my shoulder as I opened and closed the door.

Only reply I got was a grunt and a dismissive wave of her hand.

As I slid into my whip, I hit Andrea on the text. Since it was already twelve minutes after one, I knew she was at work. She figured I was laying low somewhere, but didn't know for what, or how long. At the end of the day, she couldn't tell what she didn't know. And since I hadn't been by the house in three weeks, Andrea knew it was serious.

I called every day though. Lately, I'd been making sure to talk to my son AJ more often. Of course, I had to go through Andrea's mother to talk to him. And that was a whole other obstacle in itself.

A couple years back, some shit went down. A few niggas had been tripping in front of Andrea's apartment. We weren't living together at the time, but she called me. Long story short, one of the dudes got hit in the leg. Even though I wasn't on the scene, they still charged me. I fought it for a year and a half, until they dropped the agg and just gave me a simple assault. I did eight months' state jail.

Come to find out, the State snatched my son because Andrea wouldn't stop coming to see me while I was locked up.

I heard through the grapevine, supposedly she'd been messing with one of the niggas, and the beef was behind something she'd done. Of course, when I confronted her about it, she denied it. I wouldn't be surprised. Don't get me wrong, I do my little dirt. But it's like when she does hers, she has no respect for me or herself.

I checked my phone to see if I had any messages. Nothing. Fuck it, I'll surprise her. I knew she hadn't gone on break yet, so I rode by Carl's BBQ and picked her up a rib plate with cheesy mashed potatoes and peach cobbler—her favorite.

After placing the order, I texted her phone again. Still nothing. I ate my ribs in the car while I scrolled through my page. Once I was done, I headed up to Andrea's job.

Something was itching in the back of my brain. Even as I pulled into the parking lot, my subconscious mind was screaming at me to stop. For some odd reason, my heart began to gallop in my chest.

I rode around the parking lot. Her car was parked in her usual spot. So she is at work. A sigh of relief escaped through my lips. I maneuvered through the lot and tried to find a place to park.

As I turned onto the last row, an all-black 750Li caught my attention. I noticed an empty spot about four cars down. I hurriedly turned in.

After turning off the engine, I grabbed my phone and checked once again. Still no reply. I shook my head before slipping the phone into my pocket, grabbing the bag of food, then stepping out of the car.

As I walked down the row, I got a closer look at the Beamer and paused to admire its subtle beauty. Make no mistake, I'm not a bopper, but I do appreciate nice things. Whoever's car it was had it sitting on twenty-two-inch Lexanis. No tint on the window. Glass house!

The closer I got to the car, the more I realized there's somebody in it. The Beamer was parked with the front end in, so I walked behind the rear bumper. Even though it's none of my bidness, I clearly see a man and woman sitting in the front seat talking.

Suddenly, the female's head dove into the dude's lap. Damn, she's chewing him up—broad day, in the middle of the parking lot.

I kept it pushing and headed inside.

I made it to Andrea's workstation, and the same white girl I saw last time was there. Her name tag said Kelly. She saw me and immediately offered up an explanation.

"She just went on break."

I began to ask if she knew where she went, but something in my gut told me I already knew the answer.

I about-faced and headed back out of the store. This time, I chose the row in front of the one I was parked on. That way, I could get a good look at the front end of that black Beamer.

Quickly, I crept until I was about ten feet away from the BMW. My heart triple-timed. My palms were sweaty. I knew what I'd see before I saw it. Still, I willed myself to continue forward.

I approached the back of the car that was parked directly in front of the Beamer and leaned over to the side. Now I had an unobstructed view of the front seat.

What I saw crushed me. With his head tilted back, the driver had his hand palming the back of some woman's skull. The dude—I'd never seen. The woman, on the other hand, the one who was brazen enough to be at her job sucking someone's dick, who was not her man, in a crowded parking lot, was none other than my baby momma, Andrea.

I watched in shock as she bobbed up and down into his lap. At a pace so fevered, it was as if eternal beauty was stored within his nut sack.

The shock quickly turned into anger. Then the oh-so-familiar feeling of rage kicked in. I tossed the bag of food on the ground and stalked towards my car. *Boop.*

I hit the alarm, reached under my seat, and grabbed the Glock .45 with the thirty-round dick on it. I cocked back—one slid into the head.

I began to stomp back towards the BMW. Technically, I had no beef with dude. Shit, he didn't even know me. Even if he did, his loyalty wasn't with me. So I approached the passenger-side door. At first, I thought about smashing the window. Instead, I tried the door handle.

The bitch popped open. Of course, he's the first one to spot me. Shocked and startled, he blurted out, "What the fuck?"

Andrea popped her head out of his lap, lips greasy with cock juice. She looked at me and yelled, "Oh my God!"

Chapter 12

Andrea

"Girl, I was torn the fuck up the other night," Kelly said for the third time since we'd been at work. I'm only half-listening as I type away on my phone. Today is the first day we've worked together since the lingerie party at Club Heat.

"I know," I said distractedly. "The way Tee Lee looked that night, I thought for sure your ass would have had two black eyes."

"Yea, but he ain't talking about nothing. Soon as we got back to the crib, he made me suck his dick for a whole hour before fucking me in the ass. That was his idea of punishment. After that, everything was right back peachy-keen."

"I know that's right, girl," I smirked. "Good sex makes them forget," I murmured, while trying to finish out my text message. Honestly, I wish she would just shut the hell up. Kelly was cool and all, but she had to learn to be able to read people's vibes. Didn't she see I was busy texting?

I pressed send and turned the screen off before sliding the phone into my back pocket. I do a double take. One of the customers looked familiar, but I didn't realize who it was until she was already at the counter.

"Alison, is that you, girl? Look at you, all grown up."

The last time I saw her was about a year and a half ago. She had graduated high school and was headed off to college to play volleyball.

Growing up, she used to always want to come kick it with us girls. Since all the boys were close, people expected all the girls to be close as well. But bitches don't move like niggas do. Most men have a semblance of some type of code. With women, no such code exists.

A bitch would do your hair, then suck your man's dick on the same day. I kept it cordial with the "girls," but also kept my distance. When Danielle and I went out that night, that was the first time we turnt up with each other in a long time. More than a year, in fact.

With that being said, I've always had a soft spot for her sister Alison though. She had the potential to be better than all of us.

"Yeah, it's me, Drea. I'm back from college for the summer. Actually, I've been back, going on four weeks now."

"Oh, okay. Did your sister come up here with you?"

A slight frown touched her face, but disappeared quick as it came.

"Naw, I'm up here by myself. I ain't fucking with her right now."

She began to toss the items onto the counter, along with her car keys. I noticed a miniature gold-plated shark's head dangling from the key chain. My interest piqued. Only niggas reppin' the Shark Gang were allowed to carry those. I knew four of them personally. My baby daddy was one. Another was locked away for forty years.

I nonchalantly tried to identify the make and model of the car the keys belonged to. The Dodge logo stuck out. *I wonder if this lil skank is fucking Rashard?* Her sister, Danielle, doesn't think I know she'd been fucking Rashard too. I was leaving the room with this nigga named Los, when I saw her and Rashard going in. They were pawing each other as if they were on x-pills or something. They didn't see me, but I never said anything. You never know when you may need to barter that type of information. That nigga Rah must have some good dick.

I rang up her total. $34.38. She pulled out a hundred-dollar bill, then handed it to me. I took another look at her. The glow of her skin. The way she was standing. The spread of her hips. Yeah, she'd been getting her bottom knocked out.

I handed her the change. "Girl, what's your number?" I pulled out my phone. "I know you used to always wanna come kick it with us, but your ass was too young. Now that you're grown and sexy, I could take you out and show you how Drea turns up."

"Bet," she exclaimed, happy to feel like one of the girls. As I watched her walk off, I couldn't help but notice—she even has that freshly fucked walk. I need to find out what's going on.

"Drea, who was that?" Kelly asked noisily. I damn near told her to shut the hell up and mind her own business. Instead, I kept it civil.

"That was one of my home girl's lil sister. She's a college girl, down here for the summer."

"Oh, okay. She's cute."

I resisted the urge to roll my eyes. Whatever.

"Soooo, what time are you going on break?" I asked.

Kelly looked at her watch. "Oh shit, I'm five minutes late." She scrambled to collect her things.

I watched her with amusement. "Where you headed to?"

"Girl, I don't know. Tee Lee wants to take me to lunch."

"Must be nice," I commented, just as her phone rang.

"That's him right there. Hello . . . yeah, I'm walking out the door now," she told him, as she left our workstation with some extra pep in her step.

I shook my head at the absurdity. *How could a white girl, as dingy as Kelly, snatch up a certified nigga like Tee Lee?*

I needed her to hurry up and get back off break. Mine is right after hers. We each get an hour, but management is cool. If we need to, we can add one of our fifteen-minute smoke breaks to get more time.

After pulling my phone out, I sent a quick text. The reply came almost instantly. I bit my lip and smiled. This nigga's a straight freak. I typed a quick response, then slipped the phone back into my pocket. I checked my watch for the hundredth time. Kelly needs to hurry back.

Finally, her happy-go-lucky ass came waltzing back in. Big Kool-Aid smile on her face.

"What you so happy 'bout?" I prodded.

"Nothing much. Just got some dick real quick," she bragged. I felt a slight pang of jealousy run through me.

"Girl, look at you. Nasty ass," I teased.

"Whatever," she called out, as I made my way outside to go take my break.

My phone vibrated. I checked to find a text from AD. I almost responded, but I know if I do, he'll want to talk. If I tell him I can't, or try and rush him off the phone, he'll get suspicious. Last thing I need is for him to leave wherever he's been hiding and come to my job.

For the last three weeks, AD had been ducked off. That could only mean one thing—he done got into some bullshit and needed to lay low. Call me fucked up, but I'm glad for the little break. Gave a bitch a chance to breathe.

As I neared the exit, I dialed Tee Lee's number.

"Hello?"

"Yeah, where you at? I'm 'bout to come outside."

"I'm parked on the last row. Next to Blackrock Street."

"Okay, I'm on the way."

I'll be damned if that bitch gets some of that big ole dick and I don't. I approached the passenger side of the Beamer and hopped in. The car smelled like sex, but fuck it—we 'bout to add to the aroma.

"Wassup, Drea, what you trynna do?" the nigga actually had the audacity to ask.

"Nigga, what you mean? You know damn well what I'm trynna do."

I reached for his belt and begun to unbuckle his pants. As I dipped into his boxers and gripped his dick, I felt the dryness of it. Only then did I remember they'd just had sex. I squeezed and spotted the last remnants of the nut he gave Kelly bubble up to the surface.

"My nigga, you ain't at least wash your dick off first?"

He looked at me sheepishly. "When was I going to have time? She literally just hopped out of the car ten minutes ago," he argued.

I looked at this nigga's dingy, pussy-juice-stained, dried-nut-covered dick, and I couldn't believe what I was contemplating doing.

Tee Lee sensed my weak resolve and pushed me over the edge. "You always talking that Boss Freak shit. How you're always down for whatever, however, whenever. Well, I need my dick cleaned. Ain't nothing but some pussy. Your second favorite meal."

As he urged me on, I began to stroke his piece. I shook my head in disbelief before I dove, head first. The tangy taste of Kelly's dried-up pussy juice coated my taste buds immediately.

I could smell her all in his pubic hairs. I bobbed up and down, allowing my mouth to get extremely wet, saturating his shaft. Kelly's dried-up essence began to melt away. With Tee Lee's rod looking shiny and brand new, I went into attack mode.

Ghlup—ghlup—ghlup—ghlup!

His hand palmed the back of my head. With his wide, heavy dick, he forced me to clog up my airway.

"Oooh, ssshit. That's it, you nasty freak bitch. Get that dick cleaned. Suck up that white girl's pussy juice," he taunted.

My clit thumped. My panties were soaked. My jaw ached, but I refused to let up—not until he gave me what I deserved.

His legs began to tremble. Breathing became haggard. I felt it coming—one of the biggest orgasms he'd had in a long time.

Suddenly, I thought I heard the passenger door open, but just knew I had to be mistaken. When Tee Lee hollered out, "What the fuck?" I knew then something terrible had occurred.

Reluctantly, I pulled back, allowing his dick to fall free. When I turned around, my heart stopped.

"Oh my God!"

I thought I said it in my head, but I heard myself with my own ears.

AD was standing there with a gun. The clip was long as a ruler. I didn't know what else to do but beg for my life.

"Please. Please. Baby—"

He snatched me by the back of my head, gripping my weave tightly, and yanked me out of the car with tremendous strength.

"I'm finna kill you, you nasty, slut-ass bitch!" he growled, while dragging me towards his car.

"I'm sorry. Please, AD, don't kill me, baby. I didn't mean to, it just happened."

This was the first time he'd caught me red-handed. He wasn't trynna hear none of what I was saying. This loony-ass nigga had me by the hair, tugging me at gunpoint. In the middle of the afternoon. In the crowded parking lot of a department store. And he didn't give a flying fuck.

As we got closer to his car, I heard Tee Lee call out, "Say, my nigga. Ain't no need for all that. You tripping."

AD immediately came to a halt. Without loosening his grip, he turned his body so he'd be able to address Tee Lee.

"What you just say, nigga?"

Tee Lee threw his hands up, as a show of minimal aggression. "Look, my nigga, I don't know you, and you don't know me. I know you ain't trynna get jammed up behind this shit. They got cameras everywhere, dawg. Whatever you plan on doing, you'll get caught."

Tee Lee assumed that while AD was enraged like this, he'd give a fuck about the surveillance cameras. That was the furthest thing from his mind. Matter fact, he wouldn't think about the cameras until after the fact.

I felt AD's muscles tense up. The grip he had on me tightened. I saw it about to happen before it transpired. Tee Lee made a grave mistake. He thought he was dealing with a nigga with some sense. He was about to find out the truth of the matter.

Without so much as another word, AD raised the pistol, aimed, and fired two quick shots.

Bocka! Bocka!

With a loud thud, Tee Lee dropped onto the concrete.

At the same moment, I was able to wrestle free from his grip. I took off running towards the store. I knew it was a possibility of being shot in the back, but knowing him, he'd want to look me in my eyes when he took my life. I made it to the double doors. They automatically opened, and I fled inside.

Still, I didn't feel safe until I was huddled up in the security office with David. They'd heard the gunshots, and police had been called. David had to go investigate, so he left me in the office by myself. I watched everything play out on the monitors.

I scanned through different views of the camera system and realized the location of the shooting occurred in the blind spot. They wouldn't be able to see it. My eyes darted to the monitor that watched over Kelly and my workstation. *How will I explain this to her?*

She had no idea it was her boyfriend who'd gotten shot. She assumed he was safe at home, where he said he'd be— and should have been. Her gut must've been telling her something, because I watched as she frantically kept trying to reach him on her cell phone. Over and over she dialed. Each time, the voicemail picked up.

Twenty minutes later, police entered the security office. When they asked me what happened, I told them I was in the car with a friend of mine when some unknown assailant attacked us and tried to kidnap me. My friend intervened. I heard gunshots, then ran.

When they asked for a description, I told them it happened too fast. The description I did give them was so far from what AD looked like, there would be no way someone would be able to identify him.

I know, I know. He was 'bout to kill me and I was still protecting him. Shit, that's my baby daddy. What was I supposed to do? If they don't already have him dead to rights, I wasn't 'bout to be the one to give him to them.

One of the employees must've recognized Tee Lee and knew he was Kelly's boyfriend. While the police continued to ask questions, I nonchalantly eyed a female worker approach and tell her the bad news.

Kelly's body collapsed. She hit the ground, bawling.

I don't know if Tee Lee was dead, but the way he dropped didn't look too good. I contemplated going out there and consoling her, lacing her up on my side of the story before she heard the police's version. But then I'm like, *fuck it . . . might as well leave well enough alone.*

At the end of the day, it is what it is. I'll deal with that when the time comes.

Danielle

I'm not going to work today. The baby had been kicking my ass. If I wasn't throwing up, I was breaking out in cold sweats. I grabbed my phone and tried to reach out to Alison once again. She had to have blocked me, because my call went straight to voicemail.

I knew she was alive, because she talked to Chance every day. He said she was at a friend's—some female I'd never heard about, who stayed on the other side of town. They've met up a couple times, but I guess Chance was sworn to secrecy, because he never relayed any information.

"Just tell her I love her and she could come back home anytime she wants," I told him once, when he was getting ready to go meet up with her.

Chance was supposed to head back to school the following week. Alison, a week after that. I really wanted to spend some time with her before then, but what could I do? She was grown. I couldn't make her come home.

As I sat on the couch watching Hulu, Chance came out of the bathroom smelling like fresh rain. Crisp white wife beater with some gray sweats. Even though they were loose-fitting, I still noticed the bulge in the front. I bit my lip and squeezed my thighs together, trying to suppress my primal need.

I hadn't had any dick in weeks. Because of my sudden bouts of sickness, I'm scared to go anywhere public. I was also reluctant to bring anybody home, because Chance was there. I guess that comment Alison made really hit home.

Truth be told, I hadn't been a good role model for her— parading all those different men around the house. I don't know why I thought she never noticed. Hearing that she did was a slap in the face.

As I watched Chance from the corner of my eye, my coochie dripped like a broken water faucet. My hormones were magnified, and my sex lips were sticking to my panties. *I'm not 'bout to fuck my sister's boyfriend,* I chide myself. *That would be the ultimate betrayal. But, I do need some dick, and I need it now.*

I scrolled through my phone contacts. I spotted Rashard's name and contemplated calling, but he'd been acting real weird lately. I kept searching. This young nigga from my apartments named Vic popped out at me.

Vic was my sister's age, so I never took his ass seriously. He was persistent as hell. So I took his number, mainly to shut him up. I tried finding someone else, but kept getting drawn back to Vic. I said, *fuck it,* and got at him.

Danielle: Vic. Wat u doing?

Vic: On da block. u fuckin wit a nigga?

Danielle: Yeah. Trynna c wat u got going.

Vic: Nuttin but grindn.

I took a deep breath and responded.

Danielle: U wanna cum over?

Vic: ???

Danielle: What else?

Vic: OTW!

I put the phone down and waited.

"Uhm, Chance. I'm 'bout to have some company over, but you don't have to worry, because we'll be in my room."

Chance looked at me with a smile. "That's wassup. I was starting to think you didn't want any of your friends around me."

"Boy, hush. I just ain't been feeling it lately, but something's different today. I think I can stomach some company."

Chance nodded, and I got up to go freshen myself for Vic's arrival.

Once I was done washing up, I headed back into the living room. Imagine my surprise—Vic and Chance were in the living room chatting it up like lost relatives.

"Oh shit. Danielle, I didn't know you knew my cousin Chance," Vic called out.

Cousin?

"Cousin?" The look of confusion plastered onto my face.

Chance decided to try and explain. "His mom and my dad are brother and sister. My dad moved away when I was a kid, but Vic was the one I used to always beg to go spend time with. Whenever we came down for reunions, I'd spend the rest of the summer with them."

How small can this world be?

This couldn't be any more awkward. Vic finally took notice of what I was wearing—a pair of black tights and a Baby Phat tee. He walked over and gave me a tight hug, making sure to give my ass a nice squeeze. No doubt it was for Chance's benefit as much as it was for mine.

I moaned, letting him know what type of timing I was on. "Let's go in the room," I whispered in his ear, before grabbing his hand and leading him in the room.

Soon as we entered, he wasted no time attacking my body. No subtleness. Just pure, primal need. He kissed on me hungrily. I shivered as his teeth nipped at my flesh. Goosebumps crawled up my arm. He yanked down my tights. My black thong was drenched.

Vic pulled them off delicately, exposing my juicy pussy lips sprinkled with peach fuzz. I assumed he intended to dine on my fine cuisine. Instead, he dug in his pocket, pulled out a Magnum, and sheathed himself.

I looked down. To be young, he had a nice-sized dick. About seven and a half inches, with a deep curve to it. My coochie was so wet, it dripped down the crack of my ass.

Vic lined himself up. With a great thrust, I immediately felt the tip of his cock scraping my g-spot. My breath caught in my throat. I clawed at his back as he began to beat out my box. I gripped his muscular ass, pulling him into me. Deeper and deeper.

"I'm a big girl. I can take more. Give me more of this dick," I challenged.

He raised up onto his knees, pushed my legs back until my thighs sat on my chest. With my pussy hole bussed open, Vic gave me what I craved—more dick.

I reached under my tee and popped my titties out, kneading and tweaking my nipples.

Uh—uh—uh—uh—uh! I panted, as I felt my first orgasm building.

Something moved in the corner of my vision. My bedroom door creaked open just a sliver. I spotted one of Chance's eyeballs staring at us. I locked eyes with him, letting him know I saw him—and that I was okay with him watching.

I grabbed the backs of my thighs and opened myself up even further—for the both of them.

"Open it up. Open it all the way up!" I cried out.

More to Chance, but Vic answered the call, opening my legs wider than I thought possible. My hand traveled down to my clit. I peeled my hood back and began rubbing my nub vigorously.

Vic leaned in and gave me a wet, hungry kiss. I grabbed the back of his head and held him to my chest while he worked his hips like a professional porn star.

Chance had the door wide open now. Dick in his hand, stroking for all he's worth.

I bit my lip and cried out, "Cum with me, baby. I'm finna cum. Cum with me!"

His body jerked. Creamy dick milk shot forth from his piss hole, soaking up the carpet.

Vic's body began to tremble. His muscles tensed and his cock jerked within my walls. I felt the jet stream of cum filling up the condom. Just the thought of making the young nigga's dick cum on command was too much to bear.

I dug my nails into his back and roared, "Fuuuck, I'm cuummmmiinnnng!"

My vision went black. I accidentally bit my tongue as I had one of the most intense orgasms I've ever had in my life. My body wouldn't stop vibrating.

By the time it subsided, the door was back closed and Vic was getting up to dispose of the used condom. I honestly don't know what the hell that was all about, but I hope I get a repeat before Chance goes back to school.

Chapter 13

Rashard

I was laying in bed with my eyes closed. The mattress shifted as she slid up out of bed. The scent of her pussy was still on my lips. My balls were sticky from her dew. I listened as she talked on the phone.

"Hey, baby. Yeah, Kaydon's homeboy Rashard is going to come pick me up. Then we'll come get you. Yeah, I know. I missed you too."

My eyes peeled back. Alison was standing at the edge of the bed, ass arched, looking like a Nubian goddess. Her back was towards me. She hung the phone up, then dropped her head down, as if she was feeling remorseful about something. I could probably guess.

Ever since that night she was drunk, Alison and I had been fucking like jack rabbits. Every day, all day. Turns out, while I was deep stroking her, she'd realized I wasn't her boyfriend.

"This dick is too big. It's too fucking big," she had moaned in revelation.

By then, it was feeling way too good for her to stop. Then, when she had that earth-shattering orgasm, it changed something in her. The next morning, she'd woken me up to breakfast, and when I came back in, she told me that she knew.

Honestly, I thought she was 'bout to go smooth the fuck off. Call me all types of shit, like rapist motherfucker, or perv ass nigga. Instead, she told me that was the best dick she ever had in her life, and wanted to know my intentions for her, because she had a boyfriend, for whom she loved.

Intentions? My intentions were to fuck her down. See what the pussy was like. I did. Mission accomplished. That's what I should've told her. But instead, I spun her top.

"I'm feeling you. I've been feeling you for a while, but you were just too young for me. Now that you're grown, I wanna get to know you. All of you. I'm not tripping on your boyfriend, I understand. He's number one. I'm just trynna be Mr. One Point Five."

That brought a smile to her face. She told me 'bout her being scheduled to go back to school, and wanted to know what would become of us then. *God damn, girl, slow down!* I wanted to tell her, *A nigga gave your ass some good dick, now you wanna long-term commitment?*

I won't front though. The pussy was exactly how I thought it would be. Tight, wet, fresh. So of course, I told her everything she wanted to hear. And I'd been fucking her ever since. Really, she'd turned into my own little in-house cum dumpster. Since she was supposed to be returning to school soon, I convinced her we should try any and everything we could think of. I conquered every hole she had, and had her eating my dick three to four times a day. Life was definitely good.

Now, I was supposed to take her to go scoop up her boyfriend and drop him off at the airport. I wasn't really feeling being in the car with dude, but I had promised Alison I would. Another thing I told her, just to slide up in her guts that day. *Fuck it! At least I'm about to be rid of his ass.*

She'd told him I'd be driving all the way from the East to go pick her up in Alief. Then I would drive all the way back to the East to go pick him up. Then drive all the way to the North, Bush Intercontinental Airport. Now, any sane, logical street nigga would know, I'm not about to do all that for free. And if a bitch got no money, what's the best currency?

After I hopped out of the shower, I got dressed. I overheard her call and tell him I'd just arrived at her friend's house, and we were on our way over there to pick him up. I shook my head at her duplicity. I could tell the way the lie rolled off her tongue, that wasn't the first time she ran game on him. Look at who her sister is, after all. She had one hell of a role model.

We sat around the crib and gave ourselves enough time to make the lie believable. I watched her talk to him while she sat on the couch, rocking a pair of red cotton shorts that were tight as hell. I could clearly see the outline of her camel toe. My piece began to stir.

Flashbacks of me digging all in her coochie hours before floated through my mind. She's so entrenched in her conversation, she doesn't notice when I stand up and make my way towards her. Not until my dick was poking her in the side of her face. Precum smeared over her cheek.

She covered the phone with her left hand and whispered, "No. He'll hear us."

I mouthed back, "No, he won't."

I grabbed myself at the base and rubbed my tip across her lip. She pursed her lips together in protest. But when she opened her mouth to respond to something he'd said, I was able to slip my crown in. I thought she was going to jerk back, but instead, she just sat there looking up at me. My dick head, hidden behind her pillowy lips. The rest of my piece protruding out of her mouth.

Once she saw I wasn't going to give up, she gave in. Her lips closed around my cock, and Alison began to suckle on my dick head. Lightly at first. Every so often, she'd pop me out of her mouth so she could respond to something he'd said.

I grabbed her by the back of the skull, forcing her to pay closer attention. My rod punched through her throat. Alison had no choice but to hold the phone at arm's length as I assaulted her trachea.

Awka—awka—awka—awka! Ghlup—ghlup—ghlup!

She choked on the dick, struggling for air. My balls smacked her against the chin. I could hear Chance continuously calling her name.

"Hello? Alison? You there? Hello?"

I pictured me fucking her in the ass while she wore his basketball jersey. When I came on her face, I used the jersey to wipe my dick clean. The memory was too much for me. I erupted.

My whole body locked up. My dick was the only thing moving as it spasmed, throwing up baby batter into her mouth.

"Aggghhh, fuucckkk!" I growled, trying my best not to be too loud. I didn't want to alert her unsuspecting boyfriend that the love of his life had a mouth full of my cum. Her cheeks ballooned, crammed to capacity. With one loud gulp, she swallowed my load down.

Once fully satiated, I slinked off as she licked her lips clean and continued her conversation.

"Hello? My bad, babe. I don't know what the hell was going on. I could hear you, but I guess you couldn't hear me. Yeah, I'm gonna have to definitely switch service," she finessed.

I really thought she was a good girl. I'm starting to see, she was really a wolf in sheep's clothing. I will definitely have to watch her.

After another fifteen minutes, we decided to leave the house and go scoop him up from Danielle's crib. When dude comes out, I almost feel sorry for him. The love he exhibits on his face is as real as the sun and just as hot and bright.

They gave each other great big hugs and French kisses. I looked away. I noticed Danielle standing on the sidewalk in front of her apartment. Dressed in some loose-fitting PINK shorts and a tee. Her baby bump started to show. Her arms were folded over her lactose-bloated breasts.

Even though I didn't want to deal with her at the moment, I headed her way.

"Wassup, Danielle?"

"Oh, so you do know how to still use words. For a minute there, I thought you'd become a mute."

I rubbed my face before I responded. I don't know what she wanted me to say. I don't want a baby. She does. She chose to have it, so I chose not to be around. *Simple as that.*

"I've been hella busy," I told her. "A nigga ain't dodging you. I've just been knee-deep in some shit." *Yeah, your lil sister's pussy.*

"After I drop your sister back off at her homegirl's, I'll call you," I lied.

"Uhh hmm," she snorted. She must've smelled the bullshit coming out of my pores. She took the civil route and let me get away with my lie. "Well, I do appreciate you taking Chance to the airport. Our baby's been kicking my ass. I don't know when, or where I'll be throwing up."

There she goes again with that *our* shit.

"No problem. I wasn't doing nothing." Damn, I hope she didn't notice I just contradicted myself. Earlier, I told her I was busy. Now, I claimed I was at home, not doing shit.

"Uhh hmm," she snorts again.

"Well, let me get these two lovebirds to the airport," I said, as I turned and headed back to the car. Alison and Chance are surprisingly still tongue-kissing each other. Him, grabbing two handfuls of her ass. A slight sliver of jealousy runs through me, but I quickly dissipate it. They saw me approach and Chance took it upon himself to thank me personally.

He extended his hand. I took it and shook it. "I appreciate it, Rah. For real, man."

If you knew where this hand had been an hour ago, you wouldn't be so appreciative.

"No problem, lil homie. Thank your girl. You definitely have a good one," I mocked him.

"Yeah, I know," he said proudly.

They both attempted to hop in the backseat.

"Hold up. What y'all got going on? Somebody got to sit up front, I ain't no chauffeur," I protested.

After they both looked at each other, it was decided— Alison would sit in the front seat.

Once we loaded up, I took off and hit the Beltway. Halfway there, I realized I'd forgotten to fill the tank up. I pulled over at a gas station that was connected to a burger joint and parked by the pump. I reached in my pocket and pulled out a hundred-dollar bill.

"Say Chance, do me a favor dawg, put forty dollars on pump number three, and grab me a number five with bacon on it. You want something, Alison?"

She thought about it. "Naw, I'm good."

"Well, go ahead and get whatever you want also, Chance," I told him before he hopped out of the car and headed inside.

I could tell the line at the counter was long, but so was the line in the fast food spot. As soon as I saw Chance walk into the store, my dick was back out.

Alison looked at me annoyed. "Come on, Rah, not right now. He just went into the store. What if he comes right back out?" she argued.

I wagged my piece at her. "Well, that just means you need to hurry up. Don't worry, I'll be watching. I won't let him sneak up on you."

She looked back at the store's entrance and smacked her lips in frustration. "Psshht. Uggghh."

She dove into my lap.

While Chance was in the store filling my tank up and getting me something to eat, his girlfriend was in my front seat, *eating my dick and balls.*

As she bobbed her head in my lap, I reached for the button on her shorts, unclasped them, and found my way to her tight, wet pussy. I pushed her shorts halfway down and began to finger-pop her as she chewed me up.

Ghlup — Ghlup — Ghlup — Ghlup — Awka!

She sucked my cock, eagerly wanting to swallow my cum. I kept my eyes on the store and saw Chance approaching the fast food counter, about to order my number five.

I closed my eyes and pictured fucking both sisters at the same time. That did it.

With a grunt, I held her head in place, roared, and unloaded into her mouth. For the second time, in less than two hours.

She quickly swallowed my load, pulled her shorts up, and let the windows all the way down—airing the car out.

"I can't believe you be having me doing the shit I be doing," she huffed.

"That's cause your young ass ain't never had no dick like this," I told her truthfully.

"Whatever, Rah. You got a bitch disrespecting my nigga and shit. Do you have some gum in here?"

"Naw, I don't."

She looked at me as if I was lying. Alison shook her head exasperatedly before stepping out of the car. She snatched the shorts out of her pussy crack, looked back at me one more time, then shook her head. I smelled my fingers. *Her scent was all over them.*

I watched Alison pass Chance up as she walked inside of the store. They had a brief conversation. She must've told him she needed to use the restroom, because he continued out of the store and she disappeared to the back.

By that time, I'd hopped out and began to fill the tank up. I thought he would just jump in the whip. Instead, he wanted to chat. He asked all types of questions about different shit. When he asked about Kaydon, I felt some type of way.

Damn. I hadn't realized. I hadn't heard from my nigga in over two years.

I lied and told Chance Kaydon was doing good. And that his appeal was coming along nicely. Thankfully, Chance dropped the topic after that.

Alison came back out, looking guilty as fuck. Or maybe that was just me, because I knew what she had been up to. Chance gave her a kiss before we loaded up and made the trip to the airport.

When we got there, he stepped out and came around to the driver side window.

"Once again, I appreciate it, Rah," he said, while sticking his hand out.

I shook it—with the same hand I played in his girl's pussy with.

"No problem. Like I said, lil homie, thank your girl. She's the one that convinced me too," I told him, before popping the trunk so he could get his bags out.

Alison walked him into the airport lobby. I stared at her booty and told myself, *As soon as we get back to the crib, I'm gonna fuck her in that tight, little booty hole of hers.* And that's exactly what I did.

Kaydon

"Damn, celly. I still can't believe you're finally 'bout to burn off."

My celly Hector made parole. An FI-1. By three o'clock in the afternoon, he'd be a free man. When we first became cellies, I wasn't so sure about him. He barely spoke English, and I know a lot of Pisas, and didn't take too kindly to people outside of their race.

Turns out, he's one of the realest muthafuckas I ever met. Not only did he keep it solid and not switch up on me, but he was one of the only dudes I met locked up that actually *are* who they say they are.

Because of him, I was able to lock the unit down. Flood that bitch with all types of narcotics, as well as stack a nice lil amount of bread up.

"You come right behind," he said.

"I sure hope so." My lawyer filed a motion to the court for an evidentiary hearing. I should be hearing an answer any day now.

"I'll give you a few days to get settled in, before I send Ms. Dean and Ms. T to you."

Hector frowned, as if that was the most absurd thing he'd ever heard. "No need time. I call Ms. T tonight. You should come home soon. No wait," he said, with finality.

We shook hands and I watched him walk out of the cell and off the pod for the last time.

Once he was gone, a couple of my celly's homeboys pulled up to make sure everything was still the same between us. Everybody on the unit thought that's who was getting the drops in. We'd been running that play for nine and a half months straight. No interruptions.

Shift change came. I pulled my car out the garage and dialed Claudia's number first. She didn't answer but texted back and said she was with my brother. Hit me after ten.

I dialed Ms. T up. At first, she and Ms. Dean worked the same card. After we locked them both in, I made her switch to the other card. That way, we were rocking out eight days a week. This was the last day of Ms. Dean's card, so I knew Ms. T was at the crib.

Two minutes after I texted, she replied. I told her to be looking for a call from Hector.

"He already called me. I'm on the way to go pick the pack up right now," she said.

Damn, bro wasn't playing no games.

"Text me and let me know when you make the hand-off."

"Yes, sir, Daddy," she said playfully.

I hung up and put the phone back in the stash.

I checked the time. It was after six o'clock in the evening. I put my peep mirror on the run. Sure enough, Ms. Dean was coming on the block. Lately, she'd been pressing me 'bout what my plans were if and when my case got overturned. I always told her the same thing:

"Honestly, I don't know."

She wanted a nigga to come home and shack up with her. Even though she's cool, I don't wanna go from being locked down in a cell to being locked down in a bed. The pussy was good and the head, on point. But I'll need more than that from my woman.

As she spotted my peep mirror, she smiled. I knew for a fact she'd stop by my cell during her security check walkthrough. I take a quick wash-off. Sure enough, Ms. Dean pulled right up.

"Wassup, Kay," she smirked. She knew if I'm washing up when she gets on shift, I'm looking to get up in something. Either her pussy, or her throat.

"Chillin'. My celly went to the house today. He'll be pulling up on you soon. He already tapped in with Ms. T."

"Oh yeah, that's good. When are you supposed to be heading back to the county?"

"My lawyer filed a motion three weeks ago. He said it usually takes thirty to forty-five days to grant it."

"So what, you gone let me come visit you in the County?" she asked, hopeful.

"You grown. You could do whatever you want. If you're trynna ask if I want you to come visit, then yes, I want you to come visit me, Keisha," I said, calling her by her first name.

The truth of the matter, I got a lot of love for her and her girl. They put their lives and livelihood on the line for a nigga. The trust they gave me, I didn't take lightly.

She couldn't contain her smile if she wanted to. "Okay, baby. I'll be there," she assured me, before walking off and continuing her security check.

Later on that night, while everyone was racked up, I had my homeboy Dune hold jiggers while I fucked her in the utility closet. Ms. Dean wasn't the prettiest bitch I ever ran up in, but she for damn sure had that snap back. That marshmallow pussy. *Creamy white, and extra sticky.*

As I was hitting her from the back, I looked down and saw my dick covered with a thick, white froth. Small air bubbles popped as I continued to saw into her.

Squelch — Squelch — Squelch!

Her knees buckled. She threw her hand up against the wall and braced herself. Her booty cheeks vibrated. I gripped her thighs even harder—fingertips leaving indentions in her skin.

"OH baby. I'm finna cum again. I'm finna cum again. I'm cumminngg!"

She locked onto my piece as she came all over it, for the second time in fifteen minutes. I looked down. My dick was completely submerged in white foam. My own nut began to build. I grunt.

"Fuck. I'm finna nut."

Dean pulled off my cock and turned around. With her work pants still wrapped around her left ankle, she squatted down, stuffing me into her mouth. She moaned as I bussed all in her shit.

I felt that deep suction as she swallowed deeply. My knees almost gave out. I stared down at her in amazement. I couldn't imagine how it would be once we're able to stretch out, with room to work with.

Dean lifted my piece up, lapped up under my shaft and around my nut sack. Then, after squeezing the last bit of cum out, she suckled on the head for at least half a minute. My legs trembled. I fought the urge to pry her off and allowed her to finish her ritual.

Because of her, there will be no cum stains in my drawers.

After we washed up in the sink, I let her leave out first. Ten minutes later, I followed. The rest of the night, I barely said two words to her. When she left work that following morning, I called to make sure she'd made it home safe.

The next night, Ms. T was scheduled to work. I already knew she had the pack on her, so I told the hallway's SSI to let me know what pod they assigned her to. As soon as I found out, I made my way over there to relieve her. Twenty minutes after she arrived on shift, the pack was in my possession.

I didn't have a celly yet, so I tried to hurry up, break it down, then stash the majority of it. *Hopefully, my new celly isn't a weirdo,* I thought to myself, as I sat chilling on the bunk, listening to Lo-Life's new mixtape *Chow Time Part 1: Let's Eat.*

I don't know how long she'd been standing there, but when I looked up, I saw Ms. T smirking at me. I pulled my earbuds out.

"Wassup?" I asked her, thinking something was wrong.

"I'm assuming everything went well. If not, you would've been up and down that hallway, demanding answers," she said with a smile. "Since you in here with your feet kicked up, listening to music, everything must've been put up."

"Fa shit sho. Oh, and even though I tell you this all the time, I appreciate it. I sent an extra five hundred to your app, as a token of that appreciation," I told her.

She giggled for some odd reason.

"Boy, your ass is silly. Keisha told me you're 'bout to go back to the county on bench warrant."

"Yeah, I have to have a hearing. Show my trial judge the evidence and try and convince him that I need a new trial."

She paused, as if she was about to say something but then decided against it. I prodded her along.

"What's on your mind? I know you're off your duty post."

"I am. But I'm breaking for Mr. A, so I'm good," she said.

I waited on her to open up.

172

"Look, Snow, I know you and Keisha got y'all's thing going on, and that's my girl, but I'm feeling everything about you. Your look, your walk. The way you carry yourself. I've been dropping off for you for almost a year, and I have yet to hear my name or Keisha's come up in any type of investigation. That lets me know you're a very discreet and careful man. You also made sure I got everything that was due to me, and some. Case in point, you just shot me five hundred dollars, on top of the five bands you pay for each pack."

She began to look flustered. I was surprised I was having that type of effect on her. I watched as she composed herself, then continued.

"I guess what I'm saying is, I'm trynna kick it with you when you get out. No commitment. No strings. Just two adults, having fun with each other. I just want to be in your presence. Suck up some of your energy."

I'd been known Ms. T had a thing for me. She tried her luck when she first started dropping off, but I didn't wanna cross that line. Dean and I had just begun, and I didn't wanna fuck nothing up because I couldn't control my dick.

But now that my lawyer had been paid, thanks to Claudia, I could see what Ms. T was talking 'bout.

"How do you know I'm even worth your time? I could have a small ass dick, no stroke game."

She looked at me with amusement.

"You don't think Keisha told me all about you? How you can make her cum back to back? How you touch every corner of her pussy."

"Okay, but how do you know it ain't all cap?" I asked, while sliding my hand into my commissary gym shorts.

She was about to give another retort but finally caught on, and watched the show. I stood up, took a few steps toward the bars, and pulled my piece out.

Ms. T wet her lips as she eyed my massive slab of meat. I stroked myself as I stared her down, talking to her while I jacked my dick.

"You want some of this dick right here? You think you can take all of it?"

She nodded. Her chest began to heave slightly. Her heart rate increased. As I pumped feverishly, I told her, "Tell me what you wanna do with this dick."

"Suck it. Fuck it. Put it in my ass," she whispered.

Hearing that, I jerked and spewed cum all over my fist. *Aggghh — fuck!*

She licked her lips again and couldn't take her eyes off my cum-coated hand. If I could have had her lick it off my fingers, I would. Instead, I washed my hand and dickhead in the sink before tucking myself back in.

Ms. T looked flustered. I knew her panties were soaked.

"We can definitely link up when I get out. Eventually, I'll wanna fuck you *and* Keisha," I told her, boldly.

She jerked, surprised at my request, and looked like she was about to say something, but thought better of it. Instead, she said, "I'm not tripping. If you can convince Keisha, I'm down."

I nodded, already knowing that would be the response.

We talked briefly about what she still had at the house to complete the pack. Once break was over, Mr. A came back to the pod, and Ms. T went back to hers—no doubt, with a pair of sodden panties on.

***

Later that afternoon, they finally put a nigga in the cell with me.

I immediately could tell he was a psych patient. He didn't have any appliances. His hair was nappy as fuck.

I tried to open up some dialogue and asked him how much time he had. He said, "I was supposed to get out last year, but the Marines had stormed the unit and held the Warden hostage. They made him fix my paperwork and put an extra twenty years on my time sheet. I'm trynna write the President of the United States now. Tell him they need to bring the wounded warrior home."

Yeah . . . that was the last conversation we had.

Dude pissed and didn't wash his hands. I watched him kill a roach and just leave it on the floor so the ants could come get it. I told him a couple times 'bout that shit, but it's like what I'm saying doesn't register.

It was going on the third day. I was 'bout to say *fuck it* and kick him out the cell.

Suddenly, I get a notice to pack my shit. I was on chain. Bench Warrant.

I've never been a religious man, but I closed my eyes and thanked the Lord. My lawyer said, if we could convince my judge I needed a new trial, they'd leave me in the County to wait on the Criminal Court of Appeals. If I get it dismissed or plead down to a lesser charge, I could P.I.A. out the county (*Parole In Absentia*).

I got rid of all my commissary. Depending on how long I'm gone, that shit might be old as hell when I get back. I tried to leave the legs, but Ms. Dean and Ms. T weren't having it. "If it ain't you, we ain't doing nothing," they told me when I gave them the proposition.

I can't blame them. We all ran it up, and nobody went down.

***

When I got to the County, they booked and housed me on 4B4.

It was a cool change from the hot-ass penitentiary. The females are mostly young and can't stop staring at a nigga. I'm really not sweating them. I'm more focused on touching that blacktop.

My first visit was, of course, my momma. She brought me up to speed on everything—who was doing what and with who. I specifically and *vehemently* told her not to tell anyone that I'm back in the County. I didn't need any fake "well-wishers" pulling up all of a sudden.

The next visit I got was from Claudia. Man, she looked good. Form-fitting jeans and a BCBG shirt with rhinestones on it. Her lips were coated with a light pink lip gloss.

As I stared at her mouth, I couldn't stop thinking, *Is her pussy lips as pink and shiny?*

She was so excited to see me—I would've thought she was my wife. I told her not to tell my brother shit. I didn't want anyone who abandoned me to know I would possibly be getting out. She promised she wouldn't, and that was the last time he was brought up in our conversation.

My hearing was the following day.

I was just as nervous as when I went to trial. As I laid in my bunk, trynna make myself go to sleep, I did a mental checklist on everyone who'd abandoned me.

I would make sure I got them all *Back in Blood*. I would make sure every soul on that list gets what's coming to them.

Chapter 14

AD

I'm right back at Tink's crib, hiding out.

That bitch Andrea is out of there. I can't believe I had a baby with that trick-ass hoe. Sucking some nigga's dick at her job. Yeah, she done it with me plenty of times, but *I'm* her baby daddy.

I didn't even have beef with dude. He did that to himself, jumping in my bidness with me and my baby momma. My plan was to keep it playa, snatch her ass up, but he pulled up on some Superman shit.

I don't know why niggas do that dumb-ass shit. You see a nigga handling his bitch, then it's obvious she'd gotten out of line and needed some straightening. If that was me, I would have kept on pushing. It ain't none of my bidness.

My intention was to keep it playa. Deal with the bitch, not the nigga. I guess dude called himself trynna be her knight in shining armor. These cornball-ass niggas seem to think that's the right thing to do. Well, if it *was* the right thing to do, he done it at the wrong time.

Bet he won't do that no more.

A nigga was still ducking that situation with Dame, and now this.

"*Fuck!*" I screamed out.

Tink came running from the back, in a robe and some slippers, like the house was on fire. "Boy, what's wrong with you? Why you out here screaming like you done lost your mind?"

"My bad, T, it's just—" I was 'bout to unload my problems on her, but thought better of it. "Nothing, ain't shit. A nigga just lost big on the dice game earlier. Just trynna figure out how I'mma shake back."

Tink relaxed a bit. Once she heard it was 'bout a dice game, she figured it wasn't that serious. Dice had been my addiction since before I even started fucking. "Well, you're on your own this time. I ain't 'bout to bail your ass out like I did when you were a boy," she half-joked.

She went back into her room, shutting the door behind her. More than likely, she was 'bout to blow one to the head. Out of respect for me, Tink always smoked her work in her room whenever I came over—even going as far as to put a wet towel at the bottom of the door, so the fumes wouldn't seep out.

I sat at the dining room table, trynna figure out what I was gonna do. I kept seeing dude body drop, over and over in my mind. I couldn't even say if he was dead or not. The way he collapsed, he very well may have been.

Maybe I can argue self-defense.

I quickly shook that thought from my head. A Black man with a record and an unregistered firearm? He could have shot me first, and my ass would still be going to jail.

Something caught my attention on the TV. A picture of Andrea's place of employment was on the screen. At the bottom was the caption: **Man critically shot at Department Store!**

I rushed toward the living room, grabbed the remote, and turned the volume up.

"Earlier today, a man was critically wounded after being shot by an unknown assailant. Police say they believe the victim was trynna assist a female employee who may have been in the process of being abducted."

Then, the screen cut to surveillance footage of me walking into the store. It showed me heading to the electronics section looking for Andrea. Then, it showed me leaving. Due to the angle, you really couldn't make out my face—but if you knew me, you'd recognize me.

When they showed the parking lot footage, I almost jumped for joy. Since the incident occurred in the blind spot, all you saw was me snatching Drea up and hauling her off camera. Then, my car hightailed it off the scene.

"Police ask, if you have any information concerning the possible identity of this person of interest, you're asked to contact 222-TIPS."

My heart dropped to my nuts. There it was. I'm gone.

I gripped my pistol until my knuckles turned white. The whole left side of my body began to tingle and go numb. I felt as if I was 'bout to have a heart attack or something.

I steadied my breathing. A nigga couldn't go out like that. Especially behind some fluke-ass shit.

Then, it hit me.

Andrea!

She's the key witness to everything. She had the ability to hang me out to dry. I'd like to think she wouldn't do that—that she would follow the code. But in order to follow the code, you have to have morals and principles.

What type of principles does she have, sucking dick in the parking lot of her job at one in the afternoon?

Even though it made me sick to think about it, there's no way around it. In order for me to stay free,

I had to kill my baby momma.

Danielle

"Uhh, Danielle, can you see if the customers on the patio still want their peach cobbler?"

I took a look at our manager Kadeesha and suppressed the urge to cuss her ass out. I just went outside to drop off their baked potatoes. The bitch could have said something then. Now, she wanted me to go back out there.

My feet were killing me. My back was aching, and my bladder felt like it was about to pop. I'm steady looking at the clock. Five-thirty can't come fast enough. I would've quit working, but with the baby on the way, I needed all the coins I could get.

I stepped outside and asked the older couple if they wanted to-go plates for their dessert. They said they did. So now I have to go back inside to get them, and come back outside to give them their plates. As I'm wrapping up their dessert, I catch Kadeesha side-eyeing me with a smirk on her face. I know the bitch is doing all this shit on purpose.

She was just mad because Kay curved her ass.

Years ago, Kay and I had taken a break. We'd gotten into this big-ass, monumental fight. The whole hood was talking about it. So of course, the vultures swooped in. Kadeesha was the main one. Every time Kay would pull out and go somewhere, she'd magically pop up.

One night, she couldn't take it anymore and basically took his dick. Supposedly, she went in the bathroom while he was taking a piss and gave him some head. A few days later, he and I got back together and her VIP pass had been revoked.

That was five years ago, and the bitch is still bitter about it. Oh well! I guess she felt her little position of authority constituted her getting her lick back. Not knowing, all I had to do was pull up on Carl, and her ass was done for. But I'm not no snitch-ass bitch. I fight my own battles.

I gritted my teeth and continued to pull through.

Once I dropped the dessert off, I'm about to make my way back inside when I spotted a familiar car pulling up—a burgundy Audi A8 on some twenty-inch, super poker rims. I'd know that car from anywhere. As many times as I've came on those leather seats.

Waiting for the driver to park and hop out, I paused. When he did, I was shocked to see he looked exactly the same as when I saw him last. At five foot nine inches, a hundred and ninety pounds, he wasn't a big man physically. But his aura was colossal.

Seneca and I started messing around about a year before Kay went in. I'd met him one night when Andrea, Alison, and I went out for Alison's birthday. He was definitely dripping sauce. Of course, after I took Alison back home, I let him take me to the room and fuck me down.

Our affair went on for six months, until he went to jail for some drug charges. That was over two and a half years ago.

As soon as he saw my face, he lit up. Then his eyes traveled south—to my baby bump. For a brief moment, I saw worry in his face, as if it was possible the baby could be his. Then, just as quickly, he does the math and realizes just how silly that was.

"Man. If it isn't Delicious Dee." That was his nickname for my coochie.

I blushed at the memory.

"Boy, they said you'd gotten twenty years."

"What?" He seemed shocked to hear that. "Naw, you know how these hating-ass niggas are—wishful thinking. I fought them hoes for two and a half years and ended up getting the cases dropped. I've been home about three days now."

"Oh yeah? That's good to hear. Welcome home," I said sincerely. "Where you at? Still in the same spot?"

"Naw, I lost that crib while I was gone. My girl Crystal was supposed to be paying the mortgage. I left her ass fifty bands just for that. Instead, she fucked the bread off. So now, I'm staying in a condo downtown, until I've copped something nice."

Hearing how nonchalant he was about his girl fucking off fifty bands had my pussy wet. *Momma used to say, 'You can tell the caliber of the man, not by how he acts when he gains the money, but how he acts when he loses it.'*

"Sooo—" He pointed to my baby bump.

"Oh, yeah. I don't know what I'm having yet, but I want a boy. I raised my sister Alison, and I don't need another slit and set of tits running around the house thinking she's the baddest bitch in the castle."

He smiled. I remembered those pearly whites, and those full lips, as they latched onto my clit. Pulling on my button, to and fro, until I came all over them.

"Damn. So, now that you got a bun in the oven, is the shop closed?"

"Boy, cut it out. You know you got a master key. For you, this shop's never closed," I said seductively.

Seneca wet his lips. "Bet then. Let me get your contact and we can link up tonight. I know that pregnant pussy gone be fire."

"Fa shit sho," I agreed.

We exchanged numbers, and I took his order. Seneca gave me some newfound vigor. I couldn't wait to clock out—but now, for a different reason.

When quitting time finally got there, I rushed home and took a nice, hot bath. I dropped a cap of vinegar and lemon juice in my bathwater. I used scented lotion and made sure my most sacred areas had a faint scent of hundred-dollar perfume.

After making sure my crib was equally clean and smelling good, I called him up.

Thirty minutes later, he was at my door. Ten minutes after that, his dick was in my mouth.

Seneca and I fucked each other like long-lost soulmates. He kept telling me how wet my pussy was and how he couldn't wait to come inside it. So I let him. At least three different times.

After two and a half hours, we're all sexed out, and he was preparing to leave.

He spotted a picture of Kay, which I kept on the entertainment center. It was of the last time we went out together. Even though Seneca didn't know Kay personally, he remembered him from our time messing around with each other.

"I know you're happy that your boy finna come home," he said, as he sat the picture back down.

It took my brain about a half-second to catch up. At first I thought he was talking about somebody else, so I asked,

"Who? Kay?"

He pointed to the picture. "Yeah. That's the nigga you been fucking wit, right?"

"Yeah, that's his name. But Kay got forty years. He ain't coming home no time soon."

Seneca gave me a look—one that I know all too well. The *obviously-you-haven't-been-holding-your-nigga-down* look.

"D, that nigga's in the County. My last day of court, he was going down there wit' me. At first, I didn't recognize him. He got his weight up. He's like twenty pounds heavier. I recognized the tattoo of the shark on his neck though."

My heart boomed in my chest. I couldn't breathe. I began hyperventilating.

Kay's back in the County? No . . . it can't be. Rashard would've said something. His mom would've said something.

"Are you sure it was him?" I had to ask.

"D, I'm sure. Dude wasn't exactly a peon out here. He did have a lil name for himself. I'm saying, how you don't know your nigga had a hearing on his appeal?"

I couldn't even answer that. Instead, I looked away, trying to escape his judgmental glare. When he saw I refused to answer, he continued.

"I overheard his lawyer say the judge recommended relief."

My head snapped back in his direction. I couldn't believe it. Kay was coming home? *Naw, I needed to hear that from a reliable source.*

I saw Seneca out the door, hopped in my car, and sped towards Ms. Lavella's home. No lie, I was nervous as hell. I hadn't talked to the woman since Kay got shipped off to the pen. Now, I'm 'bout to pop up at her doorstep with a whole baby in the oven. I'd be lucky if she didn't cuss me out. But I had to know.

When I pulled up, I called her phone first. Luckily, she answered.

"Hello?"

"Ms. Lavella, I'm outside your house. I really need to speak to you about something important."

She got quiet. I could've almost heard the gears in her head clicking and turning.

"Sure. I'll be out in a second."

I'm kind of peeved she didn't invite me in, but I don't let it get to me though.

Lavella came outside in a light green robe, tied around her waist, with a pair of matching slippers on. She looked at me as if I was interrupting something important. After glancing at my baby bump accusingly, she shook her head in shame.

"What's wrong, Danielle?"

I was so in a rush to get over here, but now that I'm standing in front of her, I don't know how to approach the subject.

Fuck it. I just came right out and said it.

"I just heard Kay's back in the County."

Lavella's eyebrows climbed, but she didn't think the accusation absurd. Yet, she said it was.

"Girl, that's crazy. Don't you think I would have known if my only child was in the County jail?"

I'm confused, so I don't say nothing for about five seconds. I just stared at her, studying her features, trynna detect any signs of duplicity.

But then I realized, this is a woman who came up in the streets—running game on everyone she came in contact with. Men, women, hustlers, squares. Whoever, whenever, however.

"Yeah, you're right. If he was, everybody would have known about it," I concede.

"Is there anything else?"

"Oh. Naw, Ms. Lavella. Sorry to bother you."

"It's alright."

She simply turned around and walked back inside the house.

I sat in the car and thought about it. Seneca was dead set that who he saw was Kay. Now, Kay's mom is saying that it can't be. After a few minutes of turning the problem over in my head, I decided to ride with Ms. Lavella. There was no way that could have been Kay. The whole hood would have known about it.

I cranked the car up and headed back home. I hadn't even washed my ass yet. I needed a hot shower and a good night's rest. Even though I'd decided to let it go, the mere thought of him coming home shook me. My hands were still trembling.

Kay was definitely one man I didn't want to face.

Andrea

"Ms. Palmer, we need you to cooperate with us. You said you cared about Terrence—well, this is your chance to help us catch the killer."

I'm looking at Detective Gordon like she's got to be the stupidest bitch alive. Especially if she thought I was gonna rat. And *especially* if she thought I was gonna rat on my baby daddy.

"Detective. I already told you, I don't know who it was that tried to abduct me. I was sitting in the car with Terrence, talking, when dude opened the car with a gun and tried to snatch me out. There are plenty of people who get kidnapped and don't know who their captors are," I pointed out.

"Okay, but the description you gave us clearly doesn't match the suspect on the security cameras," she pointed out.

"Well, maybe that isn't him then."

Gordon looked at me with annoyance and contempt. She knew I was lying through my teeth but couldn't prove it. It had been five days since the incident. Terrence had been on life support but died sometime last night.

So, here I was. Homicide Division on Navigation Road.

The first one to question me was an old white man with blue eyes and a hooked nose. They saw that didn't work, so they sent in a Black chick. *Psshht.* Who the fuck they think they're dealing with?

I know one thing—I've been here going on five hours, and they need to charge me with something or let me the fuck go.

"Excuse me, Ms. Gordon, but I don't see why y'all have me still here. It's going on five hours. I have a son to take care of. I nee—"

"Ms. Palmer. We know very well your mother has custody of your son. If you would have, we would have already made arrangements to revoke your rights," she interrupted.

Her ethnic background came out of her then.

I don't respond. There's no need to. It was clear—they were going to release me when they got ready.

Detective Gordon left.

I reflect quickly on how my life has changed in the blink of an eye. I haven't spoken to AD since that day, but I knew for certain he was pissed. I didn't know what the hell was wrong with me.

I have to be a nymphomaniac.

I just can't get enough dick. It didn't matter how good a nigga put it on me—soon as he was gone, a few hours later, I'd be back fiending for some more.

Maybe I need to see a specialist.

The door to the investigation room popped open. A male officer I hadn't seen before poked his head in and told me I was good to go home.

Just as I rounded the corner, headed down the stairs that lead to outside, I saw Kelly. I froze.

She watched with red-rimmed eyes. The disappointment of my betrayal was evident. This was the first time we'd laid eyes on each other since the incident.

They gave me two weeks off at the job, citing *"traumatic experiences."* And I planned on taking every day of it.

Kelly saw me, but didn't speak. No doubt she'd already discovered the truth. Tee Lee was in the car with me before he died.

As she walked right past me, I reached out and tried to grab her shoulder—attempting to get her to stop and talk to me—but she wasn't trying to hear it.

Some of the officers were now staring, smirks covering their faces. I guess they expected to see some *Jerry Springer*-type of shit popping off.

Better not.

I followed Kelly down the stairs and waited until we got outside to speak my piece.

"Kelly. Kelly! Please, wait up."

Instead of responding, she checked her phone to see how long the Uber would be until it arrived.

Fuck it. If she didn't want to speak, I'd just say what I had to say and leave it at that.

"Look, Kelly, I don't know what you think, but this wasn't that. Him and I were talking 'bout surprising you. He wanted to get you an engagement ring and needed my help to pick one out."

I don't know what the hell made me come up with that audacious-ass lie. As soon as I said it, I regretted it.

Kelly snapped her head my way.

"You filthy, lying-ass bitch," she growled through her teeth. "They gave me his property when he was in the hospital. I went through his phone and found videos of you playing in your nasty, blown-out pussy. Now you want to stand there and tell me y'all were discussing marriage plans for us? *Bitch, go fuck yourself!*"

I reeled back as if slapped in the face. I wanted to say something, but my voice caught in my throat.

I don't know why I felt bad—I barely knew the bitch. To be honest, it's probably because I didn't really have any friends. The ones I *did* have, I probably fucked their men, and now we weren't friends anymore.

Kelly was someone who genuinely wanted to be my friend.

I didn't say anything. Just stared at the Uber as it pulled up.

Right before she hopped in, she said over her shoulder, "Mark my words, Andrea—you gone pay for this. Karma's gonna spank your ass. And when it does, remember, *you did it to yourself.*"

With that, she jumped in the Uber. I watched as the brake lights disappeared down the street.

Her parting words haunted me all the way home.

Rashard

"Rah, what do you think I should wear tonight? Skirt and a blouse, or maybe a low-cut, thigh-high dress?"

Alison had both outfits laid out on the bed. She stood in front of me, nothing on but a black satin thong. I'm honestly not the right one to ask about women's fashion advice. To me, clothes looked better off than on.

Still, I humored her. "Go with the dress. I think it's sexier."

She smirked, bit her lip, then walked up and gave me a wet, passionate kiss.

"This is our last night together. I want to make sure it's special," she whispered, lips tightly pressed against mine.

I reached around and cuffed her ass cheeks. They felt heavy, but soft in my hands. My dick began to stir. I wished we had time, but we're already running late. We had dinner reservations for nine; afterwards, we headed to the club. It was 8:35 p.m.

I reluctantly detached myself and got on her ass about the tardiness.

"Alison, we gotta hurry up and get going. Our reservations are for nine. We were supposed to have been on the road."

"Okay, okay. I'mma just slip the dress on. I already did my makeup, so I'll be good to go."

Luckily, we were in the car and on our way ten minutes later. Due to my expert driving, we made it to the restaurant with three minutes to spare.

As we ate, I couldn't stop staring at her. She was a bad bitch dressed down. But as I witnessed her dressed up, she was a supermodel, Hollywood bad. Part of me wished she didn't have to go back to school so soon. She brought out another side of me. *Oh well.*

"Will you come see me?" she asked out of nowhere.

"Huh? You want me to come up to your dorm room?"

She nodded, while spearing a piece of fish with her fork, then putting it in her mouth.

"When?"

"Whenever. Just make sure it's weekends and holidays. Knowing you, I won't get any rest, and I don't want to have to miss any classes."

She had a point. I couldn't seem to keep my hands off her. Every time we get within three feet of each other, I attack. She made me feel like I was twenty years old again.

"Well, I won't make any promises," I teased, "but I'll try."

We finished our meals and headed out west to Club Heat. It was jam-packed. Every summer, Club Heat threw a Back to Class Bash. It was all for the college students who were headed back to school for the semester. It was always lit, but that night seemed more lit than usual.

I tried to valet, but they were fully booked. I dropped Alison off at the front, then left to find a place to park.

As soon as I stepped out, it was as if a gun went off—dudes from all over the parking lot stopped and stared.

The black silk dress she had on was damn near see-through. Her titties were sitting up like they had perfect posture. Her makeup, flawless. She was just oozing sex appeal.

I walked back up front, expecting to see her being harassed by multiple dudes. Instead, she stood alone, waiting on my return.

The look in her eyes when she saw me scared the hell out of me. I don't know if it was love. I hope not. I was definitely not the type of nigga she needed. All I could be is the nigga she wanted.

We entered the club and had a blast. I'm not an avid trick, but I bought her a bottle of Ace of Spades so she could turn up if she wanted.

I sat back and watched her work. She threw that ass in a circle, twerked, then dropped down and got her eagle on. I watched in admiration as dude after dude tried to handle her dance moves—only to get thrown off the saddle.

Trust me, fellas, I know how hard those hips buck, I mused to myself, as she threw it back at them.

I checked the time. 1:37 a.m.

I headed to the restroom to piss. As I stood at the urinal, a dark-skinned cat filled the stall next to me. I tried not to pay too close attention to him, but it was something familiar about him. I just couldn't put my finger on it. I knew I didn't know him personally. Still, I couldn't shake the feeling that we'd met before.

"Is that your girl out there? The one in the black dress?"

I damn near missed the comment. Only reason I realized he was speaking to me is because we were the only two in the restroom. I wasn't trying to hold a conversation with a strange man while he had his dick in his hand.

"Huh?"

"The chick that's out there, turnt up right now. Is that your girl?" he asked again.

"Yeah, you can say that," I finally answered, shaking the excess piss from the tip of my dick.

"She's bad. I gotta tilt my hat to you."

I walked off and went to wash my hands. I heard him flush and head to the sink to do the same thing. As we stood side by side, the odd feeling increased. As I glanced at him through the mirror, my Spidey senses began to tingle. He didn't say anything else, but it was as if he was daring me to recognize him.

A chill went up my spine. *Why is he asking 'bout Alison?*

Unexplainable panic took hold of me. I made a dash toward the door, but before I made it out of the bathroom, I heard him say,

"Take care of her, Cuz. You don't want to lose a bitch like that. It would be hard to find another."

Cuz?

No, no, no, no!

I ran out of the bathroom and searched frantically for her. I grabbed the waitress.

"Aye, excuse me. Did you see my girl? The one I bought the bottle for?"

The light-skinned bottle girl thought about it for a second.

"Uhh yeah. She just walked out of the club with two dudes."

Fuck!

I bulldozed through the heavy crowd, trying desperately to make it to the exit. I heard cussing and threats as I pushed and shoved, but I didn't pay them any mind.

As soon as I stepped outside, I heard the screams.

"Help! Somebody please help me!"

I scanned the parking lot, searching for the source. Twenty feet away, I spotted her—two niggas draped in dark blue, manhandling her. Even though she's petite, she was putting up a fight. One that I'm pretty sure they weren't expecting.

With no time to go and grab my pole, I looked around for some type of weapon. I spotted an empty champagne bottle on the ground, scooped it up, and ran toward their direction.

I just prayed I made it there in time. If they got to their straps, we might both be dead.

Kay

I was sitting on my bunk, legs couldn't stop bouncing up and down. Anxiety riddles my body. I stood and walked around the dayroom for the hundredth time. Even though my lawyer assured me I'd be released in a few hours, there was still a part of me that had doubts. Maybe they'll pull a tech and revoke my motion to P.I.A.

The time on the kiosk read 3:10 p.m. I should have been tired, but I was far from it. I barely slept a wink the night before. All I kept thinking 'bout was those that had done me wrong. The same ones I'd put my life on the line for. In the two and a half years I'd been gone, not one of them checked in on me. My momma and Claudia were the only two.

So now that I'm 'bout to touch the blacktop once again, all I could think about is what I would do when I laid eyes on them. The excuses they were sure to come up with. For these last couple of years, I've been patiently plotting and waiting.

When I used to get those letters from my T-Lady, telling me how my niggas were doing their best shit, my head used to hurt I was so angry. I couldn't get fifty dollars on my books, but y'all can buy bottles and make it rain on strippers in the club.

I don't even wanna start on that bitch Danielle. Supposedly, she done got pregnant on a nigga. I couldn't help but wonder who her baby daddy was.

"Snow . . . 282 . . . Snow, ATW!"

My heart leapt with excitement nanoseconds before the rest of the tank erupted. They all knew my story. How I took the charge for my niggas. And how I fought the state and gave that shit back. I'd become an inspirational story for all of them. Especially the ones that were set to go to trial. If I could do it, they could do it.

Damn near everyone bombarded me with hugs and handshakes. Even those I barely spoke to when I was on the tank.

I was finally able to make it out of the double doors. I left everything behind except for my paperwork and a few snacks. Even though I had no appetite, I munched on the Flaming Hots and waited in the process. Less than two hours later, I was walking out the front door.

I looked for her car. It didn't take me long to locate it. I remembered when it was bought. Technically, I'm the one that picked the color out—red! I began walking toward Claudia's cherry red Porsche Cayenne. After my mom told me she had to work and couldn't get out of it, I called Claudia. Luckily, she was off and delighted to come get a nigga.

She saw me approaching, hopped out, and gave me a great big hug. Claudia practically melted in my arms. Her Chanel fragrance invaded my nostrils. Before I knew it, I was gripping and squeezing her ass. I didn't intend to. But there I was, cuffing my brother's wife's booty in a downtown parking lot.

My dick began to rise. I knew she felt it poking her in her stomach. She moaned and dug herself further into my embrace, holding on to me that much tighter. Neither one of us seemed to want to let the other go.

Finally, we had to.

Reluctantly, we hopped inside her truck.

"Where do you want to go first?" she asked.

I looked at her silky smooth thighs. Her white Ralph Lauren skirt, riding eight inches above her kneecaps. I cuffed my dick and began to have wicked thoughts.

My brother flashed across my mind. I remembered us playing cops and robbers. How we used to pretend to be Stone Cold Steve Austin and The Rock. Rock Bottoms and Stone Cold Stunners were being administered all throughout the house.

Then, images of us being older. Me, looking up to him. When he rocked the gold chains, grills, and drove his slab through the hood. Many of his friends stated, "Harrell was the hardest hustler they'd ever seen."

Bitterly, I remembered the last time he spoke to me on the phone. I practically begged him for his help.

"I don't know 'bout you, Bear Claw, but I'm trynna hit the room. I'm trynna see how sweet and juicy that bear claw really is."

This was the first time one of us actually said out loud what had been on both of our minds. I wasn't sure how she would react, but wasn't surprised when she hit me with a sexy smile, bit her lip, and said,

"Harrell gets off at ten tonight." She looked at her Gucci wristwatch he bought for her last birthday. "We've got about six hours. I hope that's enough time."

"If it's not, we'll just have to pick back up on another day."

I saw the relief in her eyes. She didn't know what she wanted for us, but was glad I was willing to make it an ongoing thing until we could figure it out.

I placed my hand on her right thigh, inching my way up her skirt. As she drove us to the room, I made her buss her first nut of the day—all over my fingers.

Now that the Game God has blessed me with the gift of revenge, I wouldn't stop until everyone felt his wrath.

To Be Continued . . .

Lock Down Publications and Ca$h Presents
Assisted Publishing Packages

Due to an increase in the price of services we have increased our prices. The prices below reflect the price increase as of 11/1/24.

BASIC PACKAGE $699 Editing Cover Design Formatting	UPGRADED PACKAGE $1000 Typing Editing Cover Design Formatting Upload eBooks to Amazon Upload Paperback to Amazon
ADVANCE PACKAGE $1,400 Typing Editing (line editing/content) Cover Design Formatting Copyright Registration Proofreading Upload eBooks to Amazon Upload Paperback to Amazon	LDP SUPREME PACKAGE $1,700 Typing Editing (line editing/content) Cover Design Formatting Copyright Registration Proofreading Set up Amazon Account Upload eBooks to Amazon Upload Paperback to Amazon Advertise on LDP's Amazon and Facebook Page

***

Other services available upon request.
Additional charges may apply

Lock Down Publications
P.O. Box 944
Stockbridge, GA 30281-9998
Phone: 470 303-9761
Email: lockdownpublications@gmail.com

Submission Guideline

Submit the first three chapters of your completed manuscript to ldpsubmissions@gmail.com. In the subject line add **Your Book's Title**. The manuscript must be in a Word Doc file and sent as an attachment. Document should be in Times New Roman, double spaced, and in size 12 font. Also, provide your synopsis and full contact information. If sending multiple submissions, they must each be in a separate email.

Have a story but no way to send it electronically? You can still submit to LDP/Ca$h Presents. Send in the first three chapters, written or typed, of your completed manuscript to:

LDP: Submissions Dept
P.O. Box 944
Stockbridge, GA 30281-9998

DO NOT send original manuscript. Must be a duplicate.
Provide your synopsis and a cover letter containing your full contact information.

Thanks for considering LDP and Ca$h Presents.

NEW RELEASES

BLOODLINE OF A SAVAGE 1-3
THESE VICIOUS STREETS 1-3
RELENTLESS GOON 1-3
BY PRINCE A. TAUHID

THE BUTTERFLY MAFIA 1-3
BY FUMIYA PAYNE

A THUG'S STREET PRINCESS 1&2
BY MEESHA

CITY OF SMOKE 3
BY MOLOTTI

GET IT IN SLUGS 1 &2
BY B. STALL

STANDING ON HER BUSINESS 1&2
BY DG SANTANA

STEPPERS 1,2&3
THE REAL BADDIES OF CHI-RAQ
BY KING RIO

THE LANE 1&2
BY KEN-KEN SPENCE

THUG OF SPADES 1&2
LOVE IN THE TRENCHES 2
CORNER BOYS
BY COREY ROBINSON

TIL DEATH 3
BY ARYANNA

BACK IN BLOOD | LO-LIFE

THE BIRTH OF A GANGSTER 4
BY DELMONT PLAYER

PRODUCT OF THE STREETS 1-3
BY DEMOND "MONEY" ANDERSON

NO TIME FOR ERROR
BY KEESE

MONEY HUNGRY DEMONS 1-2
BY TRANAY ADAMS

HUB CITY MENACE 1-3
BY J. WHITE

A THUGGISH PASSION 1&2
LAND OF DA HOOLIGANZ 1-4
KILLAZ ON STANDBY 1&2
BY IRA B.

FO'EVA ROLLIN 1&2
BY ASSA RAYMOND BAKER

THE LEVEL UP 1&3
BY LUXURY KING

Coming Soon from Lock Down Publications/Ca$h Presents

IF YOU CROSS ME ONCE 6
ANGEL V
By Anthony Fields

A THUGS STREET PRINCESS 3
By Meesha

CORNER BOYS 2
By Corey Robinson

THA TAKEOVER
By Keith Chandler

BETRAYAL OF A G 2
By Ray Vinci

SAVAGE FAMILY EMPIRE 1&2
SOULLESS GOON 1,2&3
THE DIRTY SIDE OF MONEY 1,2&3
By Prince

FOR MY ENEMY'S SAKE
AMBITIONS OF A SLIDER
FRESH OFF DA PORCH
By IRA B.

BY THE TRUCKLOAD 1-4
TIPPIN' THE SCALES 1-3
BAD BITCHES WIT GUNZ 3
PROBLEM SOLVED 2
By Christopher "Diesel" Hornezes

Available Now

RESTRAINING ORDER 1 & 2
By **CA$H & Coffee**

LOVE KNOWS NO BOUNDARIES 1-3
By **Coffee**

RAISED AS A GOON I, II, III & IV
BRED BY THE SLUMS I, II, III
BLAST FOR ME I & II
ROTTEN TO THE CORE I II III
A BRONX TALE I, II, III
DUFFLE BAG CARTEL I II III IV V VI
HEARTLESS GOON I II III IV V
A SAVAGE DOPEBOY I II
DRUG LORDS I II III
CUTTHROAT MAFIA I II
KING OF THE TRENCHES
By **Ghost**

LAY IT DOWN I & II
LAST OF A DYING BREED I II
BLOOD STAINS OF A SHOTTA I & II III
By **Jamaica**

LOYAL TO THE GAME I II III
LIFE OF SIN I, II III
By **TJ & Jelissa**

IF LOVING HIM IS WRONG...I & II
LOVE ME EVEN WHEN IT HURTS I II III
By **Jelissa**

PUSH IT TO THE LIMIT
By **Bre' Hayes**

BACK IN BLOOD | LO-LIFE

BLOODY COMMAS I & II
SKI MASK CARTEL I, II & III
KING OF NEW YORK I II, III IV V
RISE TO POWER I II III
COKE KINGS I II III IV V
BORN HEARTLESS I II III IV
KING OF THE TRAP I II
By **T.J. Edwards**

WHEN THE STREETS CLAP BACK I & II III
THE HEART OF A SAVAGE I II III IV
MONEY MAFIA I II
LOYAL TO THE SOIL I II III
By **Jibril Williams**

A DISTINGUISHED THUG STOLE MY HEART I II & III
LOVE SHOULDN'T HURT I II III IV
RENEGADE BOYS 1-4
PAID IN KARMA 1-3
SAVAGE STORMS 1-3
AN UNFORESEEN LOVE 1-3
BABY, I'M WINTERTIME COLD 1-3
A THUG'S STREET PRINCESS 1&2
By **Meesha**

A GANGSTER'S CODE 1-3
A GANGSTER'S SYN 1-3
THE SAVAGE LIFE 1-3
CHAINED TO THE STREETS 1-3
BLOOD ON THE MONEY 1-3
A GANGSTA'S PAIN 1-3
BEAUTIFUL LIES AND UGLY TRUTHS
CHURCH IN THESE STREETS
By **J-Blunt**

CUM FOR ME 1-8
An LDP Erotica Collaboration

BACK IN BLOOD | LO-LIFE

BLOOD OF A BOSS 1-5
SHADOWS OF THE GAME
TRAP BASTARD
By **Askari**

THE STREETS BLEED MURDER 1-3
THE HEART OF A GANGSTA 1-3
By **Jerry Jackson**

WHEN A GOOD GIRL GOES BAD
By **Adrienne**

THE COST OF LOYALTY 1-3
By **Kweli**

BRIDE OF A HUSTLA 1-3
THE FETTI GIRLS 1-3
CORRUPTED BY A GANGSTA 1-4
BLINDED BY HIS LOVE
THE PRICE YOU PAY FOR LOVE 1-3
DOPE GIRL MAGIC 1-3
By **Destiny Skai**

A KINGPIN'S AMBITION
A KINGPIN'S AMBITION II
I MURDER FOR THE DOUGH
By **Ambitious**

TRUE SAVAGE 1-7
DOPE BOY MAGIC 1-3
MIDNIGHT CARTEL 1-3
CITY OF KINGZ 1&2
NIGHTMARE ON SILENT AVE
THE PLUG OF LIL MEXICO 1&2
CLASSIC CITY
By **Chris Green**

BACK IN BLOOD | LO-LIFE

A GANGSTER'S REVENGE 1-4
THE BOSS MAN'S DAUGHTERS 1-5
A SAVAGE LOVE 1&2
BAE BELONGS TO ME 1&2
A HUSTLER'S DECEIT 1-3
WHAT BAD BITCHES DO 1-3
SOUL OF A MONSTER 1-3
KILL ZONE
A DOPE BOY'S QUEEN 1-3
TIL DEATH 1-3
IMMA DIE BOUT MINE 1-6
DYING FOR LIKES
By **Aryanna**

A DOPEBOY'S PRAYER
By **Eddie "Wolf" Lee**

THE KING CARTEL 1-3
By **Frank Gresham**

THESE NIGGAS AIN'T LOYAL 1-3
By **Nikki Tee**

GANGSTA SHYT 1-3
By **CATO**

THE ULTIMATE BETRAYAL
By **Phoenix**

BOSS'N UP 1-3
By **Royal Nicole**

I LOVE YOU TO DEATH
By **Destiny J**

I RIDE FOR MY HITTA
I STILL RIDE FOR MY HITTA
By **Misty Holt**

BACK IN BLOOD | LO-LIFE

LOVE & CHASIN' PAPER
By **Qay Crockett**

TO DIE IN VAIN
SINS OF A HUSTLA
By **ASAD**

BROOKLYN HUSTLAZ
By **Boogsy Morina**

BROOKLYN ON LOCK 1 & 2
By **Sonovia**

GANGSTA CITY
By **Teddy Duke**

A DRUG KING AND HIS DIAMOND 1-3
A DOPEMAN'S RICHES
HER MAN, MINE'S TOO 1&2
CASH MONEY HO'S
THE WIFEY I USED TO BE 1&2
PRETTY GIRLS DO NASTY THINGS
By **Nicole Goosby**

LIPSTICK KILLAH 1-3
CRIME OF PASSION 1-3
FRIEND OR FOE 1-3
By **Mimi**

TRAPHOUSE KING 1-3
KINGPIN KILLAZ 1-3
STREET KINGS 1&2
PAID IN BLOOD 1&2
CARTEL KILLAZ 1-3
DOPE GODS 1&2
By **Hood Rich**

THE STREETS ARE CALLING
By **Duquie Wilson**

STEADY MOBBN' 1-3
THE STREETS STAINED MY SOUL 1-3
By **Marcellus Allen**

WHO SHOT YA 1-3
SON OF A DOPE FIEND 1-4
HEAVEN GOT A GHETTO 1&2
SKI MASK MONEY 1&2
By **Renta**

GORILLAZ IN THE BAY 1-4
TEARS OF A GANGSTA 1/&2
3X KRAZY 1&2
STRAIGHT BEAST MODE 1&2
By **DE'KARI**

TRIGGADALE 1-3
MURDA WAS THE CASE 1-3
By **Elijah R. Freeman**

SLAUGHTER GANG 1-3
RUTHLESS HEART 1-3
By **Willie Slaughter**

GOD BLESS THE TRAPPERS 1-3
THESE SCANDALOUS STREETS 1-3
FEAR MY GANGSTA 1-5
THESE STREETS DON'T LOVE NOBODY 1-2
BURY ME A G 1-5
A GANGSTA'S EMPIRE 1-4
THE DOPEMAN'S BODYGAURD 1&2
THE REALEST KILLAZ 1-3
THE LAST OF THE OGS 1-3
By **Tranay Adams**

MARRIED TO A BOSS 1-3
By **Destiny Skai & Chris Green**

BACK IN BLOOD | LO-LIFE

KINGZ OF THE GAME 1-7
CRIME BOSS 1-4
By **Playa Ray**

FUK SHYT
By **Blakk Diamond**

DON'T F#CK WITH MY HEART 1&2
By **Linnea**

ADDICTED TO THE DRAMA 1-3
IN THE ARM OF HIS BOSS
By **Jamila**

LOYALTY AIN'T PROMISED 1&2
By **Keith Williams**

YAYO 1-4
A SHOOTER'S AMBITION 1&2
BRED IN THE GAME
By **S. Allen**

TRAP GOD 1-3
RICH $AVAGE 1-3
MONEY IN THE GRAVE 1-3
CARTEL MONEY 1&2
By **Martell Troublesome Bolden**

FOREVER GANGSTA 1&2
GLOCKS ON SATIN SHEETS 1&2
By **Adrian Dulan**

TOE TAGZ 1-4
LEVELS TO THIS SHYT 1&2
IT'S JUST ME AND YOU
By **Ah'Million**

BACK IN BLOOD | LO-LIFE

KINGPIN DREAMS 1-3
RAN OFF ON DA PLUG
By **Paper Boi Rari**

THE STREETS MADE ME 1-3
By **Larry D. Wright**

CONFESSIONS OF A GANGSTA 1-4
CONFESSIONS OF A JACKBOY 1-3
CONFESSIONS OF A HITMAN
CONFESSIONS OF A DOPE BOY
By **Nicholas Lock**

I'M NOTHING WITHOUT HIS LOVE
SINS OF A THUG
TO THE THUG I LOVED BEFORE
A GANGSTA SAVED XMAS
IN A HUSTLER I TRUST
By **Monet Dragun**

QUIET MONEY 1-3
THUG LIFE 1-3
EXTENDED CLIP 1&2
A GANGSTA'S PARADISE
By **Trai'Quan**

CAUGHT UP IN THE LIFE 1-3
THE STREETS NEVER LET GO 1-3
By **Robert Baptiste**

NEW TO THE GAME 1-3
MONEY, MURDER & MEMORIES 1-3
By **Malik D. Rice**

CREAM 2-3
THE STREETS WILL TALK
By **Yolanda Moore**

BACK IN BLOOD | LO-LIFE

THE STREETS WILL NEVER CLOSE 1-3
By **K'ajji**

LIFE OF A SAVAGE 1-4
A GANGSTA'S QUR'AN 1-4
MURDA SEASON 1-3
GANGLAND CARTEL 1-3
CHI'RAQ GANGSTAS 1-4
KILLERS ON ELM STREET 1-3
JACK BOYZ N DA BRONX 1-3
A DOPEBOY'S DREAM 1-3
JACK BOYS VS DOPE BOYS 1-3
COKE GIRLZ
COKE BOYS
SOSA GANG 1&2
BRONX SAVAGES
BODYMORE KINGPINS
BLOOD OF A GOON
By **Romell Tukes**

CONCRETE KILLA 1-3
VICIOUS LOYALTY 1-3
BLOODY MONEY BAGS
By **Kingpen**

THE ULTIMATE SACRIFICE 1-6
KHADIFI
IF YOU CROSS ME ONCE 1-3
ANGEL 1-4
IN THE BLINK OF AN EYE
By **Anthony Fields**

THE LIFE OF A HOOD STAR
By **Ca$h & Rashia Wilson**

NIGHTMARES OF A HUSTLA 1-3
BLOOD AND GAMES 1&2
By **King Dream**

GHOST MOB
By **Stilloan Robinson**

HARD AND RUTHLESS 1&2
MOB TOWN 251
THE BILLIONAIRE BENTLEYS 1-3
REAL G'S MOVE IN SILENCE
By **Von Diesel**

MOB TIES 1-7
SOUL OF A HUSTLER, HEART OF A KILLER 1-3
GORILLAZ IN THE TRENCHES
OOPS CRY TOO 1&2
THE DAUGHTER OF A CARTEL BOSS
By **SayNoMore**

BODYMORE MURDERLAND 1-3
THE BIRTH OF A GANGSTER 1-4
By **Delmont Player**

FOR THE LOVE OF A BOSS 1&2
By **C. D. Blue**

KILLA KOUNTY 1-5
TENDER
By **Khufu**

MOBBED UP 1-4
THE BRICK MAN 1-5
THE COCAINE PRINCESS 1-10
STEPPERS 1-3
SUPER GREMLIN 1-4
A GANGSTA'S SON
By **King Rio**

MONEY GAME 1&2
By **Smoove Dolla**

BACK IN BLOOD | LO-LIFE

A GANGSTA'S KARMA 1-5
By **FLAME**

KING OF THE TRENCHES 1-3
By **GHOST & TRANAY ADAMS**

BAD BITCHES WIT GUNZ 1&2
PROBLEM SOLVED
By **"Christopher Diesel" Hornezes**

QUEEN OF THE ZOO 1&2
By **Black Migo**

GRIMEY WAYS 1-3
BETRAYAL OF A G
By **Ray Vinci**

XMAS WITH AN ATL SHOOTER
By **Ca$h & Destiny Skai**

KING KILLA 1&2
By **Vincent "Vitto" Holloway**

BETRAYAL OF A THUG 1&2
By **Fre$h**

COUNTDOWN OF A KILLA 1&2
SEX, MURDER AND GOD 1&2
GUNS DOWN, BOTTOMS UP 1&2
By **Lo-Life**

THE MURDER QUEENS 1-7
By **Michael Gallon**

FOR THE LOVE OF BLOOD 1-4
By **Jamel Mitchell**

BACK IN BLOOD | LO-LIFE

HOOD CONSIGLIERE 1&2
NO TIME FOR ERROR
By **Keese**

PROTÉGÉ OF A LEGEND 1,2&3
LOVE IN THE TRENCHES 1&2
By **Corey Robinson**

THE PLUG'S RUTHLESS DAUGHTER 1&2
By **Tony Daniels**

BORN IN THE GRAVE 1-3
CRIME PAYS
By **Self Made Tay**

MOAN IN MY MOUTH
By **XTASY**

TORN BETWEEN A GANGSTER AND A GENTLEMAN
By **J-BLUNT & Miss Kim**

LOYALTY IS EVERYTHING 1-3
CITY OF SMOKE 1-3
By **Molotti**

HERE TODAY GONE TOMORROW 1&2
By **Fly Rock**

WOMEN LIE MEN LIE 1-4
FIFTY SHADES OF SNOW 1-3
STACK BEFORE YOU SPLURGE
GIRLS FALL LIKE DOMINOES
NAÏVE TO THE STREETS
By **ROY MILLIGAN**

PILLOW PRINCESS
By **S. Hawkins**

BACK IN BLOOD | LO-LIFE

THE BUTTERFLY MAFIA 1-3
SALUTE MY SAVAGERY 1&2
By **Fumiya Payne**

THE LANE 1&2
By Ken-Ken Spence

THE PUSSY TRAP 1-5
By **Nene Capri**

DIRTY DNA
By **Blaque**

SANCTIFIED AND HORNY
by **XTASY**

BOOKS BY LDP'S CEO, CA$H

TRUST IN NO MAN
TRUST IN NO MAN 2
TRUST IN NO MAN 3
BONDED BY BLOOD
SHORTY GOT A THUG
THUGS CRY
THUGS CRY 2
THUGS CRY 3
TRUST NO BITCH
TRUST NO BITCH 2
TRUST NO BITCH 3
TIL MY CASKET DROPS
RESTRAINING ORDER
RESTRAINING ORDER 2
IN LOVE WITH A CONVICT
LIFE OF A HOOD STAR
XMAS WITH AN ATL SHOOTER